Praise for Jim Lehrer and
KICK THE CAN

"Jim Lehrer's social comedy is splendidly his own. KICK THE CAN spins freewheeling through a remarkable set of incidents—some sad, some hilarious—and moods now sunny, now dark."
EUDORA WELTY

"[A] constant pleasure ... Anybody who doesn't like this book doesn't like chicken on Sunday!"
The New York Times Book Review

"Take one part Mark Twain, add some Booth Tarkington and J.D. Salinger, try a pinch of Rabelais, and sprinkle in the spirit and sentiment of Pecos Bill and Paul Bunyan. That's the kind of rollicking, picaresque stew Jim Lehrer has fashioned!"
Chicago Tribune

"Is it a good read? You bet.... A compelling narrative voice, a knack for catching character, a whopping good sense of fun and the craft to stack up far-out episodes toward climax and insight."
USA Today

Also by Jim Lehrer:

KICK THE CAN*
WE WERE DREAMERS
VIVA MAX

*Published by Ballantine Books

CROWN
OKLAHOMA

Jim Lehrer

BALLANTINE BOOK • NEW YORK

Library of Congress Catalog Card Number: 88-22829

ISBN 0-345-36124-5

This edition published by arrangement with G. P. Putnam's Sons

Manufactured in the United States of America

First Ballantine Books Edition: March 1991

To Jamie, Lucy and Amanda

1

When It Counted

One of my duties as lieutenant governor of Oklahoma was to watch the news on national television. The governor asked me to do it for the good of the state.

"We need to know how we're doing out there, Mack," he said. "Keep that good right eye of yours looking at the television for the sights and sounds of our Sooner State."

It seemed kind of stupid at the time he said it, which was at the inaugural ball at the Park Plaza Hotel in Oklahoma City just after we had both been sworn in. I already knew how Oklahoma was doing out there. Which was great. People everywhere were humming like they were Gordon MacRae and Shirley Jones in an Oklahoma where the wind came sweeping down the plains and the corn was as high as an elephant's eye. We also had the O.U. Sooner football team, oil, the National Cowboy Hall of Fame and memories of the great Will Rogers to keep the Sooner State doing just fine out there, thank you.

But it turned out not to be stupid at all. Already noth-

ing but blessings had come to my life since I lost my
left eye, became The One-Eyed Mack and left Kansas.
Watching TV in Oklahoma ended up being another of
those blessings. A very huge blessing. Because if I had
not seen those first stories on the *CBS Evening News*
with Roger Mudd Substituting for the Vacationing Walter Cronkite, the whole Okies business could have
turned out very differently.

I don't mean to sound like a hero, because that is not
what I am. But it is straight and safe to say there's no
telling what might have happened to Oklahoma and its
people if I had not been there in front of my TV when
it counted.

Enough did as it was.

Jackie and I were in the den. We were sitting on the
leather couch I bought the year before from a furniture
wholesaler in Guthrie. Our dinner was on individual TV
trays in front of us. Jackie had brought home my favorite meal, a tunafish sandwich on toasted wheat bread
with a sack of the little narrow Fritos and a Grapette.
She had a ham-and-cheese sandwich on white bread
with mayonnaise and a Sugar Free Dr Pepper for
herself.

The children, all except for Tommy Walt, were out.
Tommy Walt told us to call him if anything important
was said on the news. He was up in his room dreaming
and praying about how to get his curve over. It would
take plenty of both, sorry to say. He was pitching for
the Oklahoma Blue Arrow Motorcoaches team, the
Buses, in the North Central Oklahoma B-Level Semi-
Pro League. He was due to start that night against the
Holdenville Lantern Manufacturing Company Green
Hornets. Unfortunately, he was not an all-star pitcher.
The problem was his fingers. They were too small to
get a good grip on the ball.

Jackie had had another tough day in her drive-thru grocery business. A thug-type kid in a red Ford pickup with Arkansas plates ran over one of the ordering stations at JackieMart–Eastside and drove off without even offering to pay for it. The senior morning stock boy at JackieMart–Westend had called in sick. And she was still in the middle of training the people at JackieMart–South Western, due for its grand opening in just three days, with me as the main speaker.

Most of my day was taken up by an oilman from Ponca City with more money and time than sense. Our governor was pushing an effort to finally get a dome built on top of our flat-topped state capitol building. The original building plans had one but the money ran out in 1915 before it got on. Ideas on how and what to do about a dome were coming in from everybody. The Ponca City oilman wanted to put a state-operated gambling casino up there to raise revenue for education and welfare. Every preacher from Assembly of God evangelists to the Catholic bishop of Tulsa was on our case about it, of course, and the idea was going nowhere. The oilman kept asking everybody when we were going to let somebody besides the preachers run things around here. When they take the vote away from the Christians, everybody replied.

I alternated night to night among the three network news programs. By a lucky chance it happened to be CBS's night. It was July and Walter Cronkite was gone. The sound of the ticker machines came up and a deep man's voice said:

"This is the *CBS Evening News* with
Roger Mudd substituting for the
vacationing Walter Cronkite."

Mudd, one of my longtime favorites, appeared in a gray suit, blue shirt and red tie and said:

> "Good evening. The activities of Organized Crime
> in this country are among the
> most difficult for lawman and
> journalist alike to penetrate. People
> who could talk don't because
> those who do often do not live long
> after they do. But CBS Justice
> Department correspondent Archibald
> Tyler has opened a significant crack
> into this
> lawless underbelly of American
> life . . . and tonight he
> has an exclusive report on a
> startling new development he found."

I took a bite of my sandwich as Archibald Tyler came up standing in front of a Washington building with a microphone in his hand. Tyler was not one of the big TV news stars people stood around Conocos and Rexalls arguing about loving or hating. If I had run into him on the corner it would probably have taken a minute or two to place even who he was and where I had seen him. But I had remembered reading something somewhere that Tyler had gone to law school.

He was puffy. His black hair was long and puffed up on his head like Elvis Presley's. His face was puffy like he didn't sleep very well at night.

But the main thing about him was his tin squeak of a voice. It sounded like a porch screen door opening.

He said there was a whole new organized crime group alive in the land. Over pictures of official-looking buildings, Italian mobsters, submachine guns and other things he said:

"Investigators believe the operations of this new Mafia competitor may be much more extensive than originally thought. In some areas, particularly in and around Kansas City, the new mob is already getting nearly thirty percent of the hard-line narcotics trade. They have also made serious inroads into the area's unions, particularly Teamster locals which had previously been the exclusive domain of the old-line Mafia. Federal agents say the reason the existence of the new group has been unknown to most Mafia leaders at the top may be that the new group has co-opted key Mafia lieutenants with payoffs—a kind of in-house organized crime brand of bribery. Officials now fear this could lead to some internal warfare within the Mafia. 'Look for some blood in barber chairs and pizza palaces,' one top investigator told CBS News. The exact nature of the new mob remains pretty much a mystery. CBS News' own sources say it is definitely an all-American group, however, with no Italian or other decided ethnic ties. It apparently has its roots in one particular section of the United States, reportedly in one specific southwestern state. Archibald Tyler, CBS News, Washington.''

Mudd said: "At the White House today, President Nixon again told congressional leaders no one on his White House staff or in his administration had anything to do with or knew anything about the break-in at the Democratic National Headquarters at the Watergate office complex in Washington. Robert Pierpoint has more.''

Pierpoint, who reminded me of the rural route postmen we had back in Kansas, went on and on about how nobody at the White House did or knew anything wrong. It was the same story he had done the week before and a couple of times before that.

Hey, Tommy Walt, get in here! Pierpoint says Nixon says nobody did or knew anything wrong!

Pierpoint finished and they went to a commercial.

"Wonder what southwestern state that other guy was talking about?" I said to Jackie as I took a sip of my Grapette.

"Are we a southwestern state?" she asked.

"Yes, ma'am."

"Sure we're not a *mid*western?"

"Sure I'm sure. I'm the lieutenant governor, please let's all remember."

"Kansas is midwestern, right?"

"Right."

"Texas is southwestern?"

"Right again."

"Why do we go with Texas instead of Kansas then? You're *from* Kansas. Why do you, as lieutenant governor, stand for Oklahoma not going with Kansas?"

"Good question."

Mudd was back with the news that the Dow Jones industrial average was off six-point-four-seven points. He did not say if that was good or bad, if we should panic or clap. They never did because we were all supposed to just know that ourselves.

Hey, Tommy Walt, get in here! Mudd says the Dow Jones closed off six-point-four-seven points! Should we sell our AT&T?

"Is it Oklahoma?" Jackie asked. She was serious.

"A Mafia in Oklahoma? No way it could be Oklahoma," I replied.

"Well, you better look into it and find out for sure," said my wonderful wife. "You really are the lieutenant governor of this state and that's your job."

It wasn't really my job to find out if there was an

Oklahoma Mafia taking over from the real other one in Kansas City and the rest of the country. But it had come up as part of my watching television. So the very least I had to do was inform the governor. That *was* my job. But that could wait until morning. The governor wasn't around anyhow. He was out in El Reno making another speech about the need to put a dome on top of the capitol.

For me tonight there was baseball. Our son was on the mound for the Buses against the Green Hornets.

Jackie did not go to the game with me because she had to go back to do some more work with her new people at JackieMart–South Western. Two of them hired to be cashiers were still having problems learning to make change for anything larger than a five-dollar bill. The young man she had hired to manage them and the store was showing signs of strain and panic. He yelled at everybody all the time. Twice he had had to go outside to his car and listen to KTOM-AM Country Rock on the radio to calm down.

"It hurts so much to watch that little thing out there pitching anyhow," she said after Mudd signed off. "It's just as well. I hate it the way they call him Trash."

I did not want to have another talk about Tommy Walt and his baseball playing. We had had more than necessary already. About a thousand more.

But she wouldn't leave it alone. "He's never going to get any better, Mack, and you know it. He's twenty-one years old and a college graduate and I think it's too much to expect that his fingers will grow any longer, don't you?"

I kissed her and she left in her tan Ford Fairlane for JackieMart–South Western.

A few minutes later, Tommy Walt came down in his home Blue Arrow Buses uniform. It was home-team white colored, with the cap, the number 12 on the back, the lettering across the front and the piping trim in Blue Arrow blue, which was dark midnight blue. The letters said: "Always Going Your Way."

He was carrying his glove and his spikes.

"Taking bets on how long the great pitcher Trash will last tonight?" he said.

"Attitude. Attitude is everything," I said.

There was the sound of a car horn out front. It was Jimmy Meeks, the Buses' good-field, no-hit shortstop. He lived four blocks away and they always rode to the games together.

"How was it at the bus depot today?" I asked Tommy Walt as he headed for the front door.

"Same as always. More one-ways than round-trips, more lost baggage than found."

"Happy pitching," I said. He probably didn't hear me but he knew I said it. I said it to him before every game.

Happy pitching. I tried to say it the way Roy Rogers used to end his TV show. Happy trails, Roy said. Happy trails. Happy pitching.

I was five feet, ten inches tall and big-boned. Tommy Walt was five feet, six inches tall and more skin than bone. That happened mostly because I was not his real father. Pepper was. Tom Bell Pepper Bowen, Jackie's first husband and my best friend. He died a Marine hero in the Korean War. Fell on a hand grenade to save the lives of his fellow Marines. They gave Jackie his medals. She was pregnant with what her doctor thought might be twins and she asked me to marry her and be her babies' daddy. It was one of the most blessed of the blessings that had come my way. I had loved Jackie as much as Pepper the minute both of us laid eyes on her back in Kansas. She chose him first. Me second. I always told her second was better than never.

Twins it turned out to be. The other one was a gorgeous and smart girl, Nancy Walterene, who was now off working as a nurse in Tulsa. We also had two other kids who were also girls who were also gorgeous and smart like their mother and were now in junior high.

Because the others were all girls Tommy Walt got all of my baseball attention. Second base had been my position when I played high school ball, before I lost my left eye. From the day he could catch and throw I naturally worked at making Tommy Walt a second baseman. He got pretty good in the field with ground balls and with making pivots and throws around the bag. His problem was judging high flies. He couldn't. And that's a killer for an infielder. It broke my heart. He also couldn't hit a curve. I had had the same problem.

So when he was a junior in high school we decided he would become a pitcher. It's easy to look back on it and say we should have stuck with the infield or switched to the outfield. But with the fly-ball and curve problems, that just did not seem like the way to go. I was not that comfortable with his becoming a pitcher. Pitchers were different. People gave them nicknames like Dizzy, Daffy, Hawk, Turk, Whip, Toothpick, Snake. They couldn't run or hit. They talked too much. They wore loud shirts. They didn't shave every day. Fine to watch but I wouldn't want my son to be one, was the way I saw it. But there was no choice. It was either pitch or quit baseball.

The baseball coach in Adabel, where we lived at the time, was a biology teacher named Alcott. He barely knew the difference between a box score and a box lunch but he said fine, and we started working on Tommy Walt's stuff. He was going to have to be a stuff pitcher. He didn't have the size or arm to overpower anybody with blazing fastballs. So it would be curves and sliders and knuckleballs and off-speed change-ups. Stuff. Some called it Trash. And soon a lot of his team-

mates started calling Tommy Walt Trash. It stuck. Jackie
blamed me for it. What could I do about it? Run out
on the diamond and threaten to whip everybody who
called my son Trash?

Tommy Walt pitched fairly well in relief all four years
at South Central Oklahoma State College while getting
his bachelor's degree in business administration. Now
he was on the mound for the Blue Arrow Buses against
the Holdenville Lantern Manufacturing Company Green
Hornets at Wiley Post Stadium.

The ballpark was cracked concrete and chipped green
paint on the state fairgrounds on the west side of Oklahoma City. It was so small the spectators felt like they
were sitting in the dugout with the players. Perfect, in
my opinion. It had been built in the late 1920s or 1930s
and was named for the famous one-eyed Wiley Post in
1944, nine years after he and Will Rogers died in an
Alaska plane crash.

Wiley Post was more than a stadium to me. He was
a special man. The librarian in Adabel named Miss
Parker told me all about him as a one-eyed Oklahoma
hero to admire and identify with. He grew up in Oklahoma and was a kid working on an oil rig here when a
sledgehammer knocked loose a piece of iron chip. It
flew up in his left eye and put it out. His employer paid
him $1,700 in compensation. Post put a white cloth
eyepatch over his empty left eye socket, bought a dam-
aged Canuck airplane with the $1,700 and went on to
international glory as an around-the-world pilot.

Wiley Post was the first famous one-eyed pilot in history, just like I was the first one-eyed lieutenant governor in Oklahoma history.

The Green Hornets were in traveling gray uniforms
trimmed in bright green. Their lead-off batter was a
right-hander who was almost as small as Tommy Walt.

Lead-off batters always are. They're up there to get on base any way they can. A walk's just fine.

Tommy Walt's first pitch was a knuckler. Head high. Ball one. An extremely slow curve, waist high, but way outside. Ball two. Ball three, a change-up in the dirt. A down-the-middle floater. Strike one. Then another knuckler head high. Ball four.

I was sitting in a box seat right behind the plate with Hugh B. Glisan, the Oklahoma Blue Arrow Motorcoaches man who managed the Union Bus Station, where Tommy Walt worked.

I yelled: "Show 'em your stuff, Tommy Walt, baby! Bear down. Show 'em your stuff, boy!"

Glisan yelled: "Hang tough, Trash! Throw your best stuff in there, Trash! Yea, Trash!"

I was glad Jackie was not there. She might have said something to Glisan. Or hit him with something.

The next batter walked on five pitches. The one after that sliced a slider to right for a double and two runs. Two more runs scored before Tommy Walt got the side out.

He didn't have his stuff. Or his trash.

The Holdenville Lantern Manufacturing Company Green Hornets were ahead, 6–0, and there were two outs in the top of the second inning. The manager, who in real life ran the Blue Arrow depot in Shawnee, walked to the mound, took the ball from him, and suddenly Tommy Walt was out of there.

And shortly afterward so was I.

I got home in time to watch the ten-o'clock news. I flipped back and forth among the three local channels to see if anybody happened to have any more on the CBS story about the new southwestern Mafia. Nobody did. Most ran the same piece of the governor's dome speech in El Reno: "It is time to complete a job undone, a job undone. It is time to raise a symbol to the heavens which says Oklahoma finishes what it starts. It is time to put a crown on our capitol. It is time to crown Oklahoma. Crown Oklahoma.'' The governor often repeated things for emphasis.

Jackie came home about ten-thirty.

"How long?" she asked.

"Top of the second," I replied.

"If he was *real* trash you'd put him in a dumpster."

"He's a pitcher."

"No, he isn't," she said.

Tommy Walt didn't come home until almost midnight. Jackie went on to bed but I stayed up in the den waiting for him. He was full of beer. Just like a pitcher.

"Drink never solved anything," I said.

"Tell that to Stan the Man," he said, and walked upstairs to his room.

Stan the Man. Stanley Frank Musial of Donora, Pennsylvania. The greatest St. Louis Cardinal in history. My favorite baseball player of all time. He now ran a swanky bar and restaurant in St. Louis. I had promised to take Tommy Walt up there sometime and buy him a steak.

2

Buffalo Joe

Our governor's real full name was Ralph Joseph Hayman but most everybody called him Buffalo Joe. Some did because he was from a small northwest Oklahoma town called Buffalo. Others did because he bore a strong resemblance to a buffalo. He had a lot of wavy dark brown hair and was six-two and paunchy and he always wore dark brown suits with black ties and white shirts.

Buffalo Joe was our forty-four-year-old man of the future. *The Daily Oklahoman* said at least once every two weeks that he was an increasingly prominent voice in the affairs of the conservative wing of the national Democratic Party. And every ten days or so he would tell me it was Oklahoma's turn in the vice-presidential sun and add something like, "I think I'm getting a tan, Mack. What do you think? What do you think?"

You bet, Joe, I always said. He insisted I call him Joe in private. Crown Oklahoma, he always replied. "Crown Oklahoma" was his shorthand slogan and password for putting that dome on the capitol. He ended all speeches and most telephone and other conversations with it, no matter the subject or whom he was talking to. Crown Oklahoma, Mr. President. Crown Oklahoma, Pope.

Our offices were right around the corner from each other in the second-floor southeast corner of the domeless capitol building, which was also the only one in the fifty states that had working oil wells on the lawn.

The governor had a suite of rooms that ran off both sides of a narrow entrance hall and reception area which led to his office at the end. His legislative, press, appointments and other people were in the offices on either side of the hall, and the closer to his office they were meant the more important they were. Naturally.

"Mack, Mack, you are here. You are here," he said, grabbing both of my hands and then my shoulders and shoving me into a chair. "How are we doing this bright Sooner morning? What does the beloved Second Man of Oklahoma have for us to ponder or digest?"

Joe had what he called an Open Mack Policy, meaning I could walk in to see him unannounced anytime I wished. That's what I had done this morning.

I told him I had been watching the *CBS Evening News* with Roger Mudd Substituting for the Vacationing Walter Cronkite last night.

"Where, where was Walter?" he asked. "We met him at last year's governors' conference. He made a speech about the freedom of the press which was mostly slop but he delivered it well. The man can talk. The man can *really* talk. Even if he's talking slop."

"They said he was gone. They called him The Vacationing Walter Cronkite."

He shook his head like it was all a puzzle to him. "We would have thought he was too important to go on vacation. Like the President of the United States or the President of Safeway. How's the Queen of the

JackieMarts, by the way? The Queen of the Jackie-Marts?"

"Great. She's doing great." Buffalo Joe's tendency to say some things twice caused me to do the same thing after I had been around him a few minutes.

"We still, we still think her drive-thru idea was one of the smartest in the history of Sooner commerce and industry," Joe said.

"We agree. We agree," I replied. He almost never said "I." He said "we." We are going to the bathroom. We love lakes. We like our hamburgers cooked medium well. We eat shrimp with our fingers. We are happy. We are sad. I had a tendency to do that same thing too, after a few minutes with him.

He was sitting behind his desk in the corner of his office. He could look out the window to the east and see the governor's mansion just two blocks away. His view to the south was of a pumping oil derrick, a wide boulevard and in the background the skyline of downtown some twenty blocks away. The derrick was a Phillips 66 which was part of a well they named Petunia #1, because it was dug through a flower bed when drilled in 1941.

The most exciting thing about his office was the red phone on the credenza behind him. It was a direct line to the warden's office at McAlester State Prison. Whenever the governor granted a last-minute pardon to a prisoner on death row he was supposed to use that phone. The first time Buffalo Joe was out of state and I was acting governor, I picked it up just to see what would happen. "This is Warden McKenzie. Is that you, Governor?" came a voice from the other end. I told him I was a telephone man checking the line. I'm hearing you loud and clear, he said. Same here, I replied, and we hung up.

I had been acting governor four times so far. The last

time was when Joe went to Williamsburg, Virginia, to that national governors' conference where Walter Cronkite spoke. There had been a lot of stories through history about nutty lieutenant governors doing nutty things while the governor was out of the state, like appointing their uncles to the Supreme Court or calling the legislature into special session to build a new highway through somebody's hometown. Nancy Walterene suggested once that I call out the Oklahoma National Guard and invade Kansas, because sunflowers made her hay fever act up. I hadn't done anything nutty. I just went into Joe's office and signed papers and took phone calls and made speeches just like he would have done if he'd been there.

Now Buffalo Joe listened as I told him about the Mafia report and the part about a southwestern state.

"Well, it sure as Texas hell is not the Sooner State of Oklahoma, we can tell you that, tell you that," he said.

"Are we sure, Joe?"

"Yes. But check it out, Mack. Check it out. Get with C. if you have to. C. would know. There may be something going on over in Tulsa we don't know about. Never have, never have trusted those people in Tulsa."

Check it out? How? Not with C., thank you. C. was C. Harry Hayes, the one-eared director of the OBI, the Oklahoma Bureau of Investigation. I did not like the man.

Joe and I talked a few minutes about what an idiotic thing the Ponca City oilman's gambling casino idea was.

"Crazy is right, and out of the question," said Joe. "But it may take a crazy idea to get our dome. We must listen to every one. Everyone. One man's craziness is another man's creativity and imagination."

We rose to leave. *I* rose to leave.

"Come by anytime," said Joe. "We always have time for the Second Man of Oklahoma."

He slapped me on the back so hard I almost fell down. "You are, you are doing work that needs to be done for this state, Mack."

"Thanks, Joe."

"The time we save not having to watch TV makes it possible for us to give the people of Oklahoma an even better governor for their money. Crown Oklahoma, Mack."

"Crown Oklahoma, Joe."

"Look at me real close here in the face, Mack. In the face."

I looked up real close at his face. At his face.

"See anything, see anything at all different?" he asked.

"The tan's getting deeper. The tan's getting deeper."

"The tan's getting deeper. You said it, Second Man. The Second Man said it. The tan's getting deeper."

Check it out? How?

I returned to my office, which was half the size of Buffalo Joe's and had only one three-foot-wide window that was way up there high on the wall. So high only a giant could see out of it.

I called my dad in Hutchinson, Kansas. He was the lieutenant in charge of the Kansas State Highway Patrol region for most of western Kansas. I had wanted to be a Kansas state trooper like him and probably would have if I had not lost my left eye. But I had no complaints about how things had worked out. Neither did dad. How many Kansas troopers have sons who grow up to be the lieutenant governor of Oklahoma?

"Yes, sir, Lieutenant Governor Son, what can I do for you?" he said so everybody in western Kansas could hear him. His voice was deep and loud like Roger

Mudd's and radio announcers'. With a little luck Dad
could have ended up as either a Vacationing or a Substituting on the news. He would certainly have sounded
better than squeaky Archibald Tyler, CBS News,
Washington.

Dad said he had never heard even so much as a whis-
per about any Mafia-like crime organization run out of
Oklahoma. But he said he would make a discreet check
with the KBI boys in Topeka and get back to me.
"KBI" stood for Kansas Bureau of Investigation.

"Missouri would be a more likely candidate, it would
seem to me," he said. "They've got every kind of hood
imaginable in Kansas City and St. Louis. There are too
many preachers and not enough money and booze in
Oklahoma. Just doesn't sound right."

"Missouri is a midwestern state. The guy with Roger
Mudd on CBS said it was a southwestern state."

"Captain Bob Peterson, you remember him from our
McPherson days, saw David Brinkley at the Kansas City
airport last March. They didn't really talk, but Bob got
his autograph for a grandson who watches a lot of TV."

The only other law enforcement officer I knew really
well was the sheriff in Adabel. He was Russell Jack
Franklin, a man the age and size of my grandfather
Wilson back in Kansas. He was very old, very fat and,
in most everybody's opinion, very crooked. There were
just too many bootleggers, card players and other as-
sorted types who always seemed to know when state
liquor or federal tax agents were about to swoop down.
Vital evidence against high-powered or big money
"Accuseds," as he called them, also had a tendency to
disappear before indictments could be returned. He
owned a blue Lincoln Continental and a white Cadillac
and a dry-cleaning plant. He bought his suits in Tulsa.

I got him on the phone right after I hung up from
talking to Dad.

"Couldn't be us," he said without thinking or pausing. "I'd know about it for sure."

"Why?"

"Because if it was that big a deal, one of their big Accuseds would have been in here trying to buy me."

"If they'd been in and made a sale, would you tell me?"

"Next question."

"What is the next question?"

"I'll check with some of the other sheriffs around. If there is such a thing as an Oklahoma Mafia one of them would know. The Accuseds couldn't operate anything big in any county if they didn't buy the sheriff. It's just that A-B-C simple."

"No sheriff's going to tell you he's been bought."

"Buying sheriffs is hard to keep secret. I'll be in touch."

Then I put in a call to Roger Mudd at CBS in New York City. I did it on a sudden impulse. It was the first call I had ever made to New York City and it was the first call I had ever made to a famous person outside the State of Oklahoma. I figured I would have no problem explaining it to the state auditor's office if I had to. The auditor was very particular about long-distance calls made on state telephones.

Roger Mudd wouldn't talk to me at first. Or at least after I asked some woman for him she went off the line for a few seconds and came back on and said Mr. Mudd was busy and could she help me. I told her again that I was the lieutenant governor of Oklahoma and what I had to discuss with Roger Mudd was of critical state security importance to my Sooner State. She asked me if I had ever met Gordon MacRae and I said no but that I did know and had actually appeared on the stage of the Orpheum Theater in Adabel, Oklahoma, once with Roy Rogers, Dale Evans, Gabby Hayes and Trigger.

She put me through.

"You have always been one of my favorite newscasters," I said to Roger Mudd in my first breath.

"Thank you, Mr. Lieutenant Governor," Roger Mudd said. "Oklahoma has always been one of my favorite states. Does the corn down there really grow as high as an elephant's eye?"

"You bet, Mr. Mudd." Very funny. I moved right on to business. "Are we the southwestern state in that Mafia story last night?"

"There's no way I could tell you that, sir, even if I knew, which I don't." He sounded just like he did on television. Like he was announcing an important cattle or land auction in southeastern Oklahoma or calling balls and strikes at Wiley Post Stadium. Or like he was my dad.

"Why not?" I said. "It is important for us to know if it is our state."

"When we know we will report it and then you will know too."

"If it is our state of Oklahoma we should be told in private, so we can go to work on putting them out of their illicit business. Stopping people from committing crimes is more important than stories on television, isn't it?"

"Look, I can't help you. It would seem to me that your own law enforcement people there in your state could find out if it's Oklahoma. Ask *them*."

"When will you have another report on the story?"

"When there's a development. Maybe tonight. Maybe tomorrow. Who knows?"

"Tonight is my night to watch NBC. I alternate among the three of you."

"Well, you have a problem then. I have to run now to tape-record a commentary for the radio. Nice talking to you, Mr. Lieutenant Governor."

* * *

Nice talking to you, Mr. Lieutenant Governor. There was something very wonderful about hearing Roger Mudd call me Mr. Lieutenant Governor.

Sometimes it was still hard for me to believe I was the lieutenant governor of Oklahoma. It happened almost like a miracle. I had been in Adabel, Oklahoma, doing my best as the youngest one-eyed county commissioner in Oklahoma history. There had been a big deal made in the newspapers about my election, because I defeated an old-time commissioner. I did it mainly because I had become a local celebrity when I went up on the Orpheum stage with Roy, Dale, Gabby and Trigger. They were in Adabel making a movie and they put on a stage show for the town before they left. They asked for a volunteer from the audience and I was picked and did very well for myself, bantering with Roy about life and myself.

The other reason I got elected was that I promised to build two war statues on the courthouse lawn. One was for the Spanish-American War dead, the other for the Korean War dead. I won and I built them. The sculptor patterned the Korean War statue after Tom Bell Pepper Bowen, my friend and Jackie's first husband. It wasn't an exact likeness by any means, but it was a Marine in battle uniform with a Browning automatic rifle and that was the important thing. It matched similar statues already on the courthouse lawn for World Wars I and II.

There had been a story in *The Daily Oklahoman* that said I might be good material for statewide office. And a few weeks later two men flew into Adabel one morning to see me on behalf of the State Democratic Committee. One was a lawyer from Woodward in the far northwestern part of the state, not far from Buffalo. His name was Arneson. The other was a Tulsa oil company executive named Heket. Arneson and Heket. *The Daily Oklahoman* called them the Party Kingmakers.

Both of them were in their forties and reminded me of late-inning relief pitchers, all full of cuteness and confidence. They said they had a private plane with its motor still running out at the Adabel airport. They had three other stops around the state before they slept in Oklahoma City that night. It was off next to see an up-and-coming county attorney in Ardmore, then a judge in Poteau and finally a state representative in Antlers.

"Understand you won the Big One in Korea," said Heket right off the bat.

"Big one what?" I replied.

"The big medal. The Congressional Medal of Honor."

"No, sir. That was my friend Tom Bell Pepper Bowen. He was killed."

"Then what's this about your wife being the wife of a Korean War hero? Didn't I read something like that somewhere?"

"She was Pepper's widow. She remarried and the person she remarried to was me."

"Does everybody know that?" asked Arneson.

"Everybody in Adabel knows."

"Has it been a problem for you?"

"Problem?"

"Politically."

"No."

"Was there anything between you and the widow before she was a widow?"

"No!"

I stood up.

Arneson and Heket stayed seated. We were in my office at the courthouse.

"We had a few more questions," Heket said.

"Please leave," I said. "I have no interest in answering any more of your questions."

"Don't you want to be a high official of the State of Oklahoma?"

"Not if it means dealing in dirt like this."

"Better we deal with it now than a newspaperman or some other dirt dealer later in a campaign," Heket said.

"We need to know everything in order to make sure we can protect you if and when you were selected to be a candidate on the slate," added Arneson.

"We don't deal in dirt," said Heket. "We bury it."

It made sense. I sat back down.

"Did you lose that eye in a war?"

"No," I said.

"Too bad," said Heket. "Wounded vets do well with the voters."

"What office do you aspire to?" Arneson asked. "There are openings this time for state treasurer, state auditor, agriculture commissioner and lieutenant governor."

"I'll take lieutenant governor," I said.

"That interests you?"

"Yes, sir."

"Why?"

"That's been my ambition."

"I've never known anybody who had an ambition to be lieutenant governor."

"Is there anything in your past that we should know about?"

"I was born in Kansas."

"We can live with that. Anything else bad, unseemly or crooked?"

"No."

"Nothing that could come along to embarrass you, the Democratic Party or the State of Oklahoma?"

There were a few things Pepper and I did when we

were traveling around together before we came to Oklahoma that I wouldn't want anybody to know about, but I just said, "No, sir." What we did was years ago, it wasn't serious and it wasn't anybody's business.

"You ever taken a bribe?" Arneson asked.

"No."

"You ever taken county or other public funds for your own use?"

"No."

"You ever thought about wearing a glass eye instead of that black patch?" asked Heket.

"Glass eyes get dirty."

"Can you wash them?"

"With Lux, yes, sir."

"You got something against Lux?"

"I like the patch."

"Some people might think it's sinister-looking," Arneson said.

"Are you saying the patch must go or no lieutenant governor?"

"No, no, Commissioner. Nothing like that. I'm just wondering what your picture will look like tacked up on a telephone pole."

"Wouldn't want the people to mix up their lieutenant governor with a wanted criminal," added Heket.

"What if instead of sinister black you wore a white patch like the great Wiley Post did?" Arneson said.

I said, "I know all about Wiley Post. He was a wonderful man. His mother and his wife made those white patches for him."

"Maybe yours could do something like that for you. Make for a good story. Young man travels the same road traveled by Wiley Post, another great Oklahoman. That kind of thing."

"My wife is too busy to sew, and my mother died in

Kansas when I was twelve, of a burst appendix,'' I said.

We were all standing now. The interview was over.

"We'll put you on the list and see what happens," said Heket.

"How long has being lieutenant governor been your ambition?" Arneson asked.

"Not long."

"What was it before?"

"I wanted to be a Kansas highway patrolman like my dad."

"We'll be in touch," said Heket.

They left for their plane with the motor running and with my motor really running.

Lieutenant governor.

I went over to the window and looked down at the statue of Private Tom Bell Pepper Bowen, USMC, on the courthouse lawn.

Pepper, how about this?

And I started laughing. Lieutenant governor of Oklahoma was what *Pepper* was supposed to turn out to be. That's why we came to Oklahoma in the first place. The point was that he could eventually pardon his father, Henry Lester (Big Bo) Bowen, when he came out of the federal penitentiary at Leavenworth after serving twelve years for bank robbery. He needed an Oklahoma pardon to keep from going directly to the state prison at McAlester for holding up a grocery store in Muskogee. It's a long story. The whole Bowen family were thugs, including Pepper, until the two of us met up on the Texas Chief streamliner and became friends. We had gone to Adabel to start a fresh life, when he got tripped up on some minor-offense arrest warrants. He went into the Marines in exchange for the dropping of all charges. Like I say, it's a long story.

I kept tabs on Big Bo, especially after I became lieu-

tenant governor. His turning up wanting a pardon could
have been a problem for me, particularly since Tommy
Walt and Nancy Walterene were technically Big Bo's
grandchildren. Fortunately Big Bo forgot about another
charge pending from Missouri, which beat Oklahoma's
to the punch. He went from Leavenworth to jail in Han-
nibal, Missouri, where he was tried and sentenced to
fifteen years for the armed robbery of a Best Western
motel managed by a retired Missouri state police tech-
nician who had the place rigged with sirens and electric
eyes and remote-controlled machine guns.

I did not hear from Arneson and Heket until four
years later. Arneson called and asked me to come up to
Oklahoma City the next Wednesday afternoon to talk
some politics. I told them I would take the Continental
Trailways up. He laughed at that and said they would
send a little private plane to get me. I told him to forget
that. I had never been on an airplane and I certainly
wasn't going to take my first plane ride on some little
private thing.

A colored guy driving a new dark blue Chrysler Imperial picked me up at the Union Bus Station at Walker
and Sheridan streets downtown. It was only the second
time I had been to Oklahoma City. The first was when
Jackie and I took the kids to the Ringling Bros. and
Barnum & Bailey Circus.

The guy in the Chrysler took me the five blocks to
the Park Plaza Hotel and then escorted me up to a suite
on the top floor. Sitting around a coffee table in huge
overstuffed chairs were Arneson and Heket and two
other men. One of the two was Buffalo Joe Hayman,
who I knew was a state senator and the Democratic
candidate for governor.

"We hear you may be just the man Oklahoma is
looking for," he said. "We are in the need of another
new Second Man, another new Second Man."

He did not have to explain. I had read all about it in the papers. The lieutenant governor nominee had retired from politics after it was revealed he had not filed a federal income tax return for fourteen years. The first chosen candidate to replace him on the slate was a thirty-four-year-old married state representative from Antlers. Three days after his selection, his unmarried nineteen-year-old secretary walked into the newspaper office in Broken Bow and announced she was pregnant. She said the lieutenant governor candidate designate was the father, but he refused to admit it or agree to support the baby after it was born. He denied the charge but said he would not run for lieutenant governor, in order to devote full time to clearing his name.

"Have you taken a bribe since we last talked?" Arneson asked.

"No. And I have still not stolen county money and I still wear a black eyepatch."

"Two new questions," said Heket. "Do you file income tax returns with the federal government and have you knocked up your secretary?"

It was a joke. Everybody laughed.

Buffalo Joe said to me, "We would, we would ask you a lot of serious questions about your background, your beliefs and your hopes and dreams for the government of Oklahoma, but Mister Arneson and Mister Heket here have already done that. They have already done that." He looked over at the two of them. "We all hope and pray they did a better job with you than they did on previous would-bes."

He stood up and offered me his hand. "We will be in touch. We will be in touch."

I caught the 2:30 express back to Adabel. The bus was a new Silver Eagle with restroom, PA system and a side destination sign. A beautiful piece of equipment.

Ten days later Heket called.

"You're it," he said. "Congratulations."

"Thank you," I said.

There were no other candidates in the Democratic primary. And I was unopposed in the general election because there were hardly any public Republicans in Oklahoma then, except during presidential elections.

So, like a sudden thunderstorm in the middle of a summer afternoon, I became the lieutenant governor of Oklahoma.

Some people kidded to my face that it wasn't a job that amounted to much. It paid $9,000 a year and I had to provide my own car and living expenses. Except for presiding over the Senate when it was in session, there wasn't even much in the way of duties or power, except on those rare occasions when the governor was out of the state. But I just reminded everyone of what one of my predecessors said in announcing as a candidate for lieutenant governor:

"When people assume the office of lieutenant governor is of no consequence, they are thinking of it in the light of honorary colonelships, admirals in the Oklahoma navy, King Bee for a day and the like. They think of it in a humorous, joking way. The office of lieutenant governor is of consequence, if for no other reason than its being an insurance policy or a guarantee that if circumstances so present themselves, Oklahoma government would continue on a sound, practical and intelligent level."

End quote, Amen and Crown Oklahoma.

Jackie had to go back to JackieMart–South Western to supervise the placing of the big electric sign outside. She was her company trademark, like Colonel Sanders was for Kentucky Fried Chicken and like Wendy was for Wendy's. The sign in front of all JackieMarts was

Jackie's smiling, beautiful face with "JackieMart Drive-Thru" lettered above it. All in color.

She had said she would stop by McDonald's and pick up dinner, so Stephanie and Cathy, our younger kids, went with her. Tommy Walt was running late at the bus depot, where he worked as a baggage agent to make himself eligible to play ball for the Buses. Semipro rules required that the players work for the team sponsor. There was also the possibility that he would make buses his career.

So I was in front of the TV all alone when it came time for the news. I had the dial on CBS. Had to. My good friend Roger Mudd said another story could run tonight or anytime.

The first story was another Pierpoint report from the White House. It was about how a White House lawyer named Dean had been asked by President Nixon to get to the bottom of the Watergate break-in story.

Second was the Mafia story. Archibald Tyler again was the correspondent. He was still standing in front of that same Washington building with a microphone in his same right hand.

He said:

"Two Mafia lieutenants turned up
    dead today in Kansas City. Both were machine-
    gunned by unknown assailants while having their
    shoes shined at a barbershop on the city's north side.
    Authorities believe the killings are
    related to the intramob warfare
    spurred on by the new competitiveness of
    a new Mafia group. CBS News
    reported the new group's existence last night. It
    is of a non–Italian, non–East Coast
    heritage. It is headquartered in a
    southwestern state. Sources said

further today that it was apparently a state known
for its football, because football
position names were used to identify
members of the mob, rather than the
traditional family terms used by
the more traditional Italian-based
Mafia. Archibald Tyler, CBS News,
Washington.''

3

Lost

The next day was a dark day for all of us.

Jackie woke up upset at six o'clock in the morning. She did not upset easily. Only when it mattered and was justified. This morning it mattered and was justified.

"I have no milk for any of the stores today. Colbert's Dairy is closed because of a fire. I have no outside string lights for tonight's opening. The electricians forgot to order them. The Skeeter Walker and the Purples band canceled because two of the Purples have the flu. I'm not sure there will even be a PA for you to talk into, Mack. The publicity didn't get out right. Nobody's coming. My manager T. Ray Powell is still crazy and he's driving everybody else crazy. Thunderstorms are forecast for this afternoon. Whatever made me think I could be a businesswoman, I do not know. I am headed for wrack and ruin."

"Buffalo Joe told me yesterday you were the pride of Sooner business and industry," I said. "Pride of Sooner business and industry."

"Did you say, 'Pride of Sooner business and industry. Pride of Sooner business and industry'?"

She almost laughed. By 6:30 she was in the Fairlane on her way to her day's destiny as founder of the JackieMarts.

Then came Tommy Walt. He was due at the bus station at 7:30, but he was still sitting at the kitchen table at 7:15.

"I hate it, Dad. There is nothing about putting baggage checks on suitcases that I find the least bit fun or rewarding. A chimpanzee could do it. It's nothing work. I hate it. I really do hate it. I am not going to do it today or anymore."

"You have to, to stay eligible to play ball," I said. "Remember the semipro rules. You have to put in at least thirty-five hours a week at the sponsor's . . ."

"I am talking about putting baggage checks on suitcases. That is all I am talking about."

"I always loved being in and around buses and bus people."

"I am not you."

It was 7:22 and he left for the bus station in his secondhand International pickup. He bought it the summer before with money he made working at an OTASCO store and playing for the Jacks, their semipro team. OTASCO stood for Oklahoma Tire and Supply Company and their stores were a lot like Western Autos. There were hundreds of them all over Oklahoma.

I got Stephanie and Cathy off to school. They were easy compared to their mother and big brother. All they wanted was not to have to eat oatmeal for breakfast. I said that was fine with me, and off they went.

And I went off to my office. I was stuck with doing the one thing I hated having to do. I was going to have to turn to C. and the OBI.

The OBI was to us in Oklahoma what the KBI was

to Kansans, what the Texas Rangers were to Texans and what the FBI was to all Americans: the last people on earth anybody ever wanted to tangle with. C. was their leader. C. Harry Hayes. C. for short, C. for Cool. There were many stories around about him. How he lost his right ear in a Nazi prisoner-of-war camp. How he had almost single-handedly brought legalized drinking to Oklahoma by enforcing the dry laws with the mass arrests of upstanding Oklahoma Baptists and Holy Roads with glasses of whiskey in their hands at upstanding restaurants and hotel coffee shops. How he made it a point to have no public officials as personal friends, because he assumed it was only a matter of time before he'd have to investigate them for stealing money, goods or votes from the people of Oklahoma.

There were rumors that he knew everything about everybody and was not reluctant to use what he knew to get what he wanted. I had met him twice—both times at big social occasions thrown by Buffalo Joe at the governor's mansion.

"This is the lieutenant governor, C.," Buffalo Joe said, introducing me the first time. "He's the lieutenant governor, C."

"Right. Son of a Kansas highway patrolman. Husband of a waitress," said C.

"That waitress is now the Second Lady of Oklahoma," I said.

"Was married to an ex-con before you."

"An ex-con who fell on a hand grenade and was blown to bits in Korea."

I wanted to tangle with this guy some more right then and there in front of Buffalo Joe and all of Oklahoma. But I restrained myself. Primarily because he had only one ear. There wasn't anything where his right ear was supposed to be but a hole and some shiny scar tissue. The story was that a Nazi prison guard seared off his ear with a hot carving knife. I was sure *The Daily Okla-homan* or *The Tulsa Tribune* or somebody would have made a big deal out of the one-eyed lieutenant governor getting into it with the one-eared head of the OBI.

C. was a tall thin man who could have passed any-where for a piece of gray concrete. His skin was gray and so were his eyes and his suit and his tie and prob-ably his heart and his soul and his mind. He was some-where between fifty and sixty years old. It was hard to tell for sure.

The second time I introduced myself as someone he had met before, the lieutenant governor of Oklahoma.

"Right. I remember. Son of a highway patrolman in Kansas," he said. "Husband of an ex-con's widow . . ."

"Who is now the owner and operator of Jackie-Marts."

"Right. I picked up a can of chicken noodle soup and some saltines at one of them the other night."

I placed the call to C. now with dread. He came on right away and definitely remembered that I was the lieutenant governor and that we had met twice before. He confirmed for the third time that I was the son of a Kansas state trooper and the husband of an ex-con's widow. I asked him to come by and see me at my office on an urgent matter that I could not discuss on the phone.

"How urgent?" he asked.

"More urgent than anything else we have going on in the State of Oklahoma at this particular moment in history."

"Doubt that. But I'm on my way."

Two young men in dark suits and white shirts walked in with him ten minutes later. Bodyguards, obviously. Maybe he expected me, the lieutenant governor of Oklahoma, to harm him.

"Do you watch television, Mr. Director?" was my

first question after he sat down in the chair across from me.

He made a motion to stand up. "You get me over here on the fetch that it's more urgent than anything else going on in our state and then you ask me if I watch television. Is the next question what are my favorite shows? Well, Mr. Lieutenant Governor, my TV habits may be a subject of urgency to you, but not to me."

"Remain calm, Mr. Director."

He looked at me like he might turn to those two young men in dark suits and white shirts and order me eliminated. He was C. C. for Cool. People did not go around telling him to remain calm.

I pressed on. "If you can spare me a few more of your precious minutes, I will prove to your satisfaction a television viewing poll is not what this is all about."

My tone was what Tommy Walt would probably have described as an "up yours." But I had figured the only way to get to this guy was to play the same kind of tough game he played. I was right.

He settled back into his chair.

"Did you see the story on the *CBS Evening News* last night about the Mafia?"

"I do not watch CBS or any other television except when I am in the hospital, in a hotel room or visiting my mother at her nursing home in Guthrie. I wasn't in any of those places last night."

"How about the night before?"

"No."

"Well, they have had a big story running the last two nights about a new organized crime ring that is giving the Mafia a run for its money and its vice, corruption and murder. They say it's based in one southwestern state. They say the state is one where football is a big deal. The governor has asked me to find out if it's Oklahoma."

"We could have handled this on the phone, Mr. Lieutenant Governor," he said with an ever so slight smile. "The answer to your inquiry is one word. No."

"No, it isn't Oklahoma?"

"Precisely."

He stood, nodded to his two young men in dark suits and white shirts, and headed for the door.

He stopped and turned around to me.

"How did you lose that eye?" he said.

"How did you lose that ear?"

I had him again. "Maybe we should get to know each other better before we exchange such personal stories," he said. He was smiling. C. for Cool was smiling.

"The word is you don't get to know public officials better," I said.

"That's a good word," he said, still smiling. "But I am willing to try an exception now and then. Don't disappoint me, Mr. Lieutenant Governor."

"Crown Oklahoma, Mr. Director."

"So The Chip's got you doing it, too." "The Chip" was another of Buffalo Joe's nicknames. It derived from buffalo chip, which derived from buffalo dung.

C. gave me a wave and left.

All parents know what's at the other end of a telephone ring. Smashed cars, mutilated or drowned young bodies, kidnapper demands and a million other tragedies and unpleasants.

Some flashed before me when Janice Alice Montgomery, my secretary, came into my office with a white face and a shaky voice to say, "It's the bus depot on the line. Tommy Walt's been in some kind of accident. . . ."

Hugh B. Glisan, the terminal manager, spoke calmly and much too slowly.

"We do not know what happened exactly, Mr. Lieutenant Governor. Trash was taking baggage at the baggage check-in window there off to the right side of the ticket counter. You know where it is, sir. When you walk in the doors there on the west side, turn left, and there it is. Well, suddenly we heard a lot of racket and yelling. He—that's Trash—was throwing baggage and express at passengers, at the porters, at the walls. One small metal case went right through the window out onto the loading dock. You know where that window is, sir, there by Dock Five. We tried to stop him peacefully, but nobody could manage and suddenly he ran off like he was being chased by the demons. I think it goes without saying, sir, that we cannot have suitcases being thrown at the passengers for very long before it begins to hurt business. . . ."

"Was he hurt?"

"No, sir."

"Was anybody hurt?"

"No, sir."

"Did you call the police?"

"No, sir."

"Where is Tommy Walt now?"

"Like I say, he ran off like he was being chased by a rabid dog. I have no idea where he went or . . ."

The bus depot was twenty-four blocks from the capitol and I was there in my Buick like a shot. I checked in with Glisan to see if Tommy Walt had shown up. He hadn't. They had picked up most everything. But I did see the broken window. I told Glisan Tommy Walt would pay for the damage.

I walked to the lot three blocks away where Tommy Walt usually kept his old pickup while at work. It was there, parked way back in the corner under the one tree that still remained in the area. I looked inside the cab. There was nothing to see.

Then I heard a human sound from the rear of the truck, from the open bed in back.

There was Tommy Walt, lying stretched out on his back, looking straight up at the good blue Oklahoma sky.

"Hi, son," I said.

"Hi, Dad," he said without looking over at me. "I told you I hated my job. I told you I did. I finally could not put one more baggage check on one more suitcase. I just couldn't. Something just snapped. I got to thinking about Mr. Arnold David Rutledge. He's the Blue Arrow general baggage agent, Dad. He's in charge of finding lost baggage. He sits at a desk in the middle of a huge warehouse down on the other side of the river. All around him are stacks of baggage. Lost baggage. Cardboard boxes of clothes and food that was checked in Altus for New York and ended up in New Mexico. Brown leather suitcases that were supposed to go to Tuscaloosa, Alabama, or Traverse City, Michigan, but went to Anadarko, Oklahoma. Big canvas duffel bags that poor sailors and soldiers checked on bus tickets to San Diego, California, and went to San Diego, Texas, or to Ardmore, Oklahoma, instead of Ardmore, Pennsylvania, Ponca City, Oklahoma, instead of Kansas City, Kansas, or God knows where else instead of. There are thousands of these things. Millions. Mr. Arnold David Rutledge opens them and looks for clues to who they belong to. Then he tries to find the owners. He's got twelve phones on a big round desk in front of him. They're all different colors. White, beige, blue, red, green, black, blue. He's talking on six at one time while the others are ringing. It's a Trailways agent in Breckenridge, Texas, looking for a black trunk that may have gone to Turner Falls, Oklahoma. Did it? Don't think so, Mr. Rutledge says. He says it sounds like a trunk that he heard about that turned up unclaimed at the Carolina Coach depot in Raleigh, North Carolina. Why Raleigh? Who knows. That's the mystery of it, Dad. We put a bag on a bus here in Oklahoma City to go to Tulsa. That's a hundred fourteen miles away. Takes our express schedules two hours on the nose, bus depot to bus depot. The bus gets there and the passenger gets there, but the bag doesn't. Two weeks later, it is found in Bismarck, North Dakota. Why Bismarck? Nobody knows, Dad. Not even Mr. Rutledge knows. Nobody can figure out what happens. Suitcases and cardboard boxes, and duffel bags and trunks and all the rest. Their baggage checks get torn off. Or the wrong checks get on the wrong bags. Or there were none on them in the first place. Some have minds of their own. Lives of their own. Travel plans of their own. The passenger may want to go to Tulsa, but the suitcase had already made plans to go to Bismarck. Mr. Arnold David Rutledge is the man who tries to work it all out. Tries to get the passenger and his baggage back together again. He's like a counselor. He tries to keep people and baggage from splitting forever. He reunites them in happiness. He spends all day in that warehouse, Dad. Opening the suitcases and boxes, talking on the phone about suitcases and boxes. I don't want to do that with my life, Dad. I do not want to be a Mr. Arnold David Rutledge. I have great respect and admiration for him and the work he does for the Oklahoma Blue Arrow Motorcoaches. But I do not aspire to take his place.''

"You don't have to, son. No, sir.''

"You know what they call Mr. Rutledge? They call him Lost. Hi, Lost. How's it going today, Lost? How's the family, Lost? Want to get a Big Mac and some fries for lunch, Lost? Lost. That's the worst nickname I have ever heard. Except for Trash. Trash is worse. Lost is a whole lot better than Trash, isn't it, Dad?''

"Not necessarily.''

"I am not crazy, Dad. I am not. It's just baggage. I don't care about it. I cannot put checks on suitcases and brown cardboard boxes and duffel bags anymore. Sitting in a warehouse surrounded by lost baggage is not my goal in life. I can't be a baggage man anymore."

"Well, you surely don't have to."

"What about baseball?"

"Maybe you've put in enough hours already. We'll check. Maybe you'll be eligible for a while. Glisan can probably find another job for you. Maybe behind the ticket counter. Now there is where the pleasure and the glory are. Behind that counter."

"Sure, Dad."

He got up and jumped over the side to the ground where I was.

"I'll go back and apologize," he said. "Maybe he'll let me stay on if I pay for the damage."

"I'm sure he will. Do you want me to go with you?"

"No, thanks. You're the lieutenant governor of Oklahoma. You've got more important things than this to do."

He headed off for the depot. I gave him a few minutes and then I walked the same way until I came to my Buick.

I was there a half-hour early and the sky to the west was already dark. Scary Oklahoma summer thunderstorm dark. It looked like it was maybe over the Clinton area, seventy-five miles or so away. That meant we had twenty to twenty-five minutes at most before it would be right here on top of Oklahoma City and the grand opening of JackieMart–South Western.

The place looked great. Particularly the JackieMart sign. Jackie's hair and eyes were both a bit darker than in real life. Her nose was a tiny bit smaller too. But that buoyancy in her beautiful face with the smile and twinkle was right on the money. The artist and the sign-maker had done a perfect job. They had put her in a red, white and blue blouse with a red kerchief. Jackie's likeness was a good eight feet high and five feet wide, so it could be seen clearly coming at it from either north or south on Western Avenue. It lit up so she sparkled and shined even more.

I told her that seeing it had given me a great idea. Why not put one on the top of the new dome of the state capitol? I promised to speak to Buffalo Joe about it as soon as possible.

Look, Joe, we could lease the space to Jackie and she could put one of her signs up there and help pay for the dome. Crown Oklahoma with Jackie. How about it, Joe? How about it, Joe?

The substitute band was a country music outfit from Guymon called The Panhandlers because Guymon was located in the Panhandle. Jackie had them set up outside in front of the main entrance ten minutes earlier than planned. She had everybody do everything ten minutes earlier than planned. Including me.

That meant the crowd was lighter than it might have been. But with the storm, there wasn't any choice. Do it early and stay dry, do it on time and get stormed on and out. I didn't count heads, but there were about thirty people standing out there when I started speaking. Maybe thirty-five. Jackie had ordered free Dr Peppers, Cokes, balloons, ballpoint pens and other giveaway things for three hundred people.

I said:

"I stand before you this afternoon in two ways proud. I am here as the proud lieutenant governor of this state, proud that another of our vital Sooner business minds has once again shown the fortitude and the genius to stake another claim. I am here as the

proud husband of that vital Sooner business mind
that has done it.''

There was a crack of lightning. I guessed it to be
about over El Reno. Yukon was next. Then Bethany and
us. We were down to about four minutes.

"Let me tell you the story of JackieMart. Once upon
a time there was a beautiful Oklahoma mother and
wife who believed there had to be an easy and better
way to pick up basic groceries. Sure, there were big
supermarkets. Sure, there were convenience stores.
But in both cases the young mother with the small
child or the husband racing home to be with his
family had to park and get out of the car. Why not
have drive-thru stores so you didn't have to get out
of the car? Why not have places where you pulled
your car to an ordering station to place your order
and then drove up to a window and picked up the
order? Why not? Thus was born the JackieMart.
JackieMart–Eastside was first. JackieMart–Westend
was next. And now—here in all of its glory—is
JackieMart–South Western.''

I felt a raindrop on my check. The bandleader handed
me a pair of scissors. There was a blue ribbon hanging
across the front of the door.

"It is with the supreme pride of a husband and a
lieutenant governor that I cut this ribbon to open
this marvelous new Oklahoma business.''

I cut the ribbon. The band played "Oklahoma!" from
the musical. The people applauded.
And we all ran for cover. I grabbed Jackie's hand and
made a dash inside.

It was a typical, normal, regular afternoon summer thunderstorm. There was pounding hail, rain and wind and enough noise to make you think the Santa Fe's Texas Chief streamliner was bearing down on JackieMart–South Western.

It was over and gone in fifteen minutes, on its way to Midwest City, Shawnee, Seminole and points east.

Within five minutes there were cars lined up at the ordering stations. JackieMart–South Western was in business.

I kissed Jackie and left. I had to get ready to watch the *CBS Evening News* with Roger Mudd Substituting for the Vacationing Walter Cronkite.

Tommy Walt watched it with me. He had gone to the Pig Stand and brought back barbecue sandwiches, chips and Dr Peppers. We had talked only a few minutes about his scene at the bus depot. But he appeared calm. Hugh B. Glisan had taken him back. On probation. But he still had to work the baggage room until a chance to train him on the ticket counter came up. There was no assurance when that would be.

It was the first story on the newscast.

Mudd introduced Archibald Tyler, CBS News, Washington. Tyler came on camera standing in front of a map of Oklahoma. I was barely breathing.

"They call themselves the Okies. All of them either are from the State of Oklahoma or have strong Oklahoma connections. Their leader goes by the name Boomer. Thus the first sketchy profile begins to emerge of the new organized crime group that is causing violence and havoc for the old-line Mafia and for law enforcement agencies from one end of the country to the other.

"CBS News, through a variety of investigative

and first-hand sources, has been able to put together the following information on the Okies:

"Their operation is so secret that many of its members do not even know the full extent of their organization. Like traditional intelligence agencies, everything is on a 'need to know' basis.

"Most of the key leaders do not have criminal records—yet. They operate—in Oklahoma and elsewhere—as seemingly reputable businessmen, labor leaders and others. Most of the leaders are known to have strong personal ties to each other. The top three Okies in the Kansas City area, for instance, were all classmates at the University of Oklahoma. They and their Okie colleagues elsewhere use legitimate businesses for laundering and hiding the proceeds of their illicit operations, a well-known practice pioneered by the old-line Mafia. The Okies' fronts include banks, union trust funds, business colleges, grocery stores, medical and dental clinics and several transportation concerns.

"The number-one Okie is reportedly in the transportation business in Oklahoma. The only other known information about him is that nickname, Boomer, apparently derived from the University of Oklahoma Sooners fight song 'Boomer Sooner.' There were reports he and several of his key lieutenant played football together, but that could not be confirmed.

"Security and loyalty within the group is so tight, law enforcement officers have had little success infiltrating it—either through placing undercover agents or through buying informers within the organization. Also, no disenchanted Okies have yet come forward to spill inside information.

"CBS News has learned the Okies' first organizational meeting was about three years ago in a small Oklahoma town southwest of Tulsa. Six of the current Okie kingpins attended that session, which lasted more than four days. Within the organization, that meeting is now fondly referred to as 'Blue Bell,' in apparent reference to a motel or other location where it actually took place.

"One final sidelight:

"The Okies reportedly have their own unique brand of titles for their people. They're based on football terminology. Instead of don or godfather, their top people are called coach or skipper. First-level lieutenants are known as quarterbacks, QBs for short. 'Running back,' 'tailback' and 'wing-back' are also used, depending on the person's specific function. Okie soldiers, on down the hierarchy line, are given lineman designations. All are from the offensive side of the line. Sources say that grows out of a basic Okie philosophy that is offensive.

"Archibald Tyler, CBS News, Washington."

I was not able to speak. Not at first. Not for a count of ten or fifteen. Finally I said, "It is a tragedy. A tragedy for Oklahoma and a tragedy for your father, the lieutenant governor of Oklahoma."

"It's not your fault, for God's sake," Tommy Walt said.

"It happened on TV while I was watching. Now I must report what I heard."

To say that I walked extremely slowly to the phone is to say the truth. I was in no hurry. No hurry at all.

The line was busy. All three lines into the governor's mansion were busy.

So I got in the Buick and headed for the governor's mansion to report to Buffalo Joe in person the awful things I had heard from Archibald Tyler, CBS News,

Washington. The mansion was just east of the capitol
and our nice brick home was on 16th, south and east of
there, down by the University of Oklahoma medical
school complex. In other words, I was only a few minutes away.

But I was too late. Joe already knew and he was crazy.

"Mack! Mack! There you are. How could, how could
you let this happen?" he yelled at me the second he
saw me. He was in a sitting room he used as an office
on the second floor of the mansion. C. Harry Hayes
was there. So were Arneson and Heket.

"I just saw it on the TV myself, Joe," I said.

"But you knew it was coming. You told us about it
beforehand. You knew it was coming, but you didn't
stop it. You told me two days ago you knew it was
coming."

Among Buffalo Joe's many tendencies was killing the
messenger. He had once fired a secretary for telling him
rain was forecast for an outdoor rally in Pawhuska. A
legislative assistant got demoted for reporting the out-
come of a vote on a sales tax hike. Buffalo Joe was
opposed to it and thought he had the votes to win in
the House. He didn't and it made him crazy. Until now
I had never suffered because I had never before delivered him news—good *or* bad.

"No, sir," I said. "What I said was that I wondered
if it was Oklahoma they were talking about. I set out
to find out. . . ."

"C. says it's a crock," Joe said. "Right, C.?"

"Precisely."

"People don't just make up things like that," I said.

"They did this time," C. said.

Buffalo Joe stood so we would know the meeting was
over. He pronounced the result. "Our position is that
we have launched an investigation of these charges. If
we find evidence of such evil in our state it will be

eliminated and purged. We will pursue the truth from Vinita to Hobart, from Waynoka to Broken Bow. From Vinita to Hobart, from Waynoka to Broken Bow . . .''

Arneson interrupted. "Better throw in a city or two, Joe.''

"I hate cities,'' Buffalo Joe said. "The worst thing that ever happened to this country and this state was when people started moving to cities. If there *is* a Mafia here, it'll be found in one of them. Probably Tulsa. You just wait and see. Probably Tulsa.''

"It's a crock, Governor,'' C. said.

"Right,'' said Buffalo Joe. "Now you and Mack here go prove it is. That is an assignment. An assignment.''

C. looked at me like having me as a partner was not the best thing that had ever happened to him. But he would make do. I felt the same way.

"Yes, sir,'' I said.

C. said, "Isn't this a matter best left to law enforcement?''

"Look what that approach has gotten us so far,'' Arneson said.

"Our state smeared on the national news is what it has gotten us,'' Heket said.

"And while Mack was watching, while Mack was watching,'' Joe said. Obviously, if *he* had been watching the news on national television none of this would have ever happened.

Crown Oklahoma, Joe.

Heket took the floor. Like he was addressing a Lions Club at noon. A few nice words here for the chairman, a story or two from his boyhood and finally a pitch for common sense and the Democratic Party in the politics and government of Oklahoma.

"Gentlemen, let me tell you what is about to happen,'' he said. "I've seen it after tornadoes and murders and everything else that makes big news. Reporters are going to come in here like locusts from New Mexico. There's not going to be a vacant Holiday Inn room anywhere in the state. Every Tom, Dick and Harry with a crackpot theory or morsel of information is going to be interviewed. Everything about us and our state will be misconstrued and mis-screwed, to coin a new one. The locusts are coming, Joe. They are coming to eat us alive and spit us out. Oklahoma will never again be like it was before CBS did it to us tonight. Never again . . .''

"Tell it to Mack here," said Buffalo Joe, who was now almost calm. "This is his project. Tell him. Tell him all about what he has let happen to our Sooner State of Oklahoma. This is your project. Right, Mack? I have had nothing to do with it. Nothing to do with it. It happened on TV, so it's yours. Right, Mack? It happened on TV.

C. and I made for the exit.

Joe did not say good-bye. He also did not say, Crown Oklahoma, Mack. Or ask me about his tan.

4

Boomer Sooner

It was not easy being the lieutenant governor of Oklahoma, a father and a husband all at that same time.

Jackie was almost happy the next morning. JackieMart–South Western had ended up having a fairly good first night. Cars were at all four ordering stations much of the entire evening. But T. Ray Powell, the young manager, was still a major disappointment. He got so nervous he started yelling at every customer who didn't have the right change. The cashiers and the stock people and all the rest rose to the occasion, thank God, and did beautifully.

Several customers wanted to know when she was going to open a JackieMart in the north part of town. There were others who requested one in Altus and Lawton and Bethany. JackieMarts had been a hit since the first one opened and they still were. Not even a thunderstorm from Clinton could change the fact that Jackie had come up with a genius idea. It was a good idea for our family, because without her income we would have had a hard time making all of our ends meet on my $9,000-a-year lieutenant governor's salary.

I was struck by what the thunderstorm almost did to her business, though. I was always struck by what the weather did. An old Thunderbird Motor Coaches bus driver who was a friend of my dad's in Kansas was responsible for the way I thought about weather. One spring, Cottonwood Creek came out of its banks, flooding out the main road and all of the secondary roads and the Santa Fe tracks south to Wichita. Santa Fe canceled its trains and Thunderbird canceled all of its buses. Dad's friend happened to drive one of the first runs through after the water went down five days later. I was at the bus station with Dad and heard the driver tell the story of a young man from Salina, Kansas, who was on his bus four days before, when it had to turn back at Newton. He was on his way to Wichita to start a new job in the accounting department of Beech Aircraft. He had been number one of three finalists for the job, and when he didn't show up they gave it to number two. The young man called them on the phone and Beech said they were sorry and they certainly did not blame him for the rain, but they simply could not wait. Maybe something else would open up some other time, they said. The young man went back to Salina. The bus driver made the point that the young man's life had been changed forever because it rained in Kansas that spring. Think about the loves and wars and fortunes and whatevers that had probably been won or lost because it snowed or rained or did whatever on any particular day. Think about it, he said. And think about it I did every time the weather turned bad.

Tommy Walt wouldn't talk to me or to Jackie or to his sisters. He ate his oatmeal and peaches and left with only a grunt for a good-bye.

"Baseball has done him in, Mack," Jackie said. "Can't you see that?"

"It's baggage that's done it," I said, and immediately wished I hadn't.

"It's the same thing," she said.

"Putting baggage checks on suitcases is not the same thing as throwing knuckle balls in the North Central Oklahoma Semi-Pro League."

"They both hurt if you don't do them well."

"He's fine at putting on baggage checks. He just doesn't like doing it."

"Same thing."

"It is *not* the same thing. Throwing a knuckler over the plate waist-high takes skill and training. Putting a baggage check on a suitcase takes none of the above."

"They call him Trash, Mack. How would you like to be called Trash?"

"I named myself The One-Eyed Mack when I left Kansas," I said. "That didn't bother me. It's the same thing."

"It is not and you know it," she said.

I walked her to her Fairlane, kissed her and sent her off to more JackieMart glory.

Then I got in my Buick and headed for Adabel to see Sheriff Russell Jack Franklin.

It was a comfortable, familiar two-hour drive. I loved getting in my car and driving down the roads of our state. Particularly on the little two-laners. I despised the big four-lane interstates and toll roads. Nobody needs to go that fast anywhere. Particularly to places like Tulsa or Texas, which is where most of our big highways ended up.

Today's trip was through Meeker, which had a big sign on the way into town which said it was the home of Carl Hubbell, one of the greatest pitchers of all time. I went past Police Cars America, Inc., a company that traded in used police cars—both marked and unmarked. They had a whole field of them with the lights still on top, the painted shield emblems still on the side. Small towns in Oklahoma and all around that could not afford brand-new big-engined, fully equipped police cruisers could afford used ones. These guys bought the old ones from Tulsa, Oklahoma City and other cities, refurbished them mechanically and otherwise, and sold them to the little guys.

I also went by the farmer who had completely encircled his place with a fence made of old tires buried upright half in the ground, and by the Sooner American Eagle Café, which boasted of having on a pole in front the largest American flag in Oklahoma. It was twice as big as any other flag I had ever seen. The owner bought it secondhand from a tire company in Ohio that flew it outside its factory during World War Two, so it had only forty-eight stars.

Normally, being in the car by myself helped me think. But not this time. I could not think of anything major or important. Not about what to do about Tommy Walt and his problem. Not about the coming of the Okies and my problem.

Russell Jack and I went for a cup of coffee at Brown's Hotel Coffee Shop. Jackie worked there as a waitress when we all first came to Adabel in 1949. Now she was the Second Lady of Oklahoma and founder of JackieMarts. Only in Oklahoma could something like that happen.

I came to see Russell Jack because I couldn't think of anything else to do and I felt I had to do something. Dad always said, Do something. Anything. Do something. So I had come to see a crooked sheriff.

He had seen the CBS report on the Okies. I told him what C. had said about it.

"He's right. It's a made-up figment."

"Those news people don't make up figments just like that," I said.

"You know better than that, Mack," he said. "Just yesterday we picked up an Accused down on the Pragueville blacktop driving a stolen car. We ran a check with the highway patrol and they ran a check with the FBI and it turned out the car was stolen in Jackson, Mississippi, last Friday. Well, it turned out everybody with a badge on has been looking for the Mad Georgia Cracker, a guy who shot and killed five people at a small grocery store in Macon, Georgia, last week. One of the five was a police officer who came upon the scene. Another was a seventy-eight-year-old woman customer. Another was a fifteen-year-old stock boy. Well, one of our deputies, a dumbbell named Lauderdale, gets it in his head that the Pragueville blacktop Accused was the Mad Georgia Cracker Accused. You know Little Jimmy Abbott, who covers the courthouse for the *Post-Times*. Well, he got wind of it and decided he had one helluva big story. We told him everything we knew and then he went back to his office to write it up. About a half-hour later, the OBI called from Oklahoma City. Wrong Accused. Wrong match. The Mad Georgia Cracker was white. Our Accused wasn't. Theirs was fifty-five years old, ours was twenty-four. Theirs was six-four, ours was five-eleven. So I picked up the phone myself and called Little Jimmy Abbott. Too late, he says. I'm already almost through with the story that says it looks like the Mad Georgia Cracker, who killed five people including a cop, an old lady and a young boy, has been arrested outside Adabel, he says. They're going to make it the lead story, he says, with a banner headline clear across the top of the front page and with his byline in big type. Well, it ain't so, I say. Well, why not wait until tomorrow to tell me, he says. It's a great story and I need it and the paper needs it, he says. Well, fine, I say. And that's that.''

"It's not the same thing," I said. "The *Adabel Post-Times* with Little Jimmy Abbott at the Courthouse is not the *CBS Evening News* with Roger Mudd Substituting for the Vacationing Walter Cronkite.''

"Yeah, it is, Mack. It's an identical match. It's exactly the same. How many times since you've been county commissioner or lieutenant governor have you read or watched or listened to a story that you knew as well as your own middle name was a dead-wrong made-up figment? . . .''

"Look, this is different.''

"All right, this is different. Then let me run through some things about this Okies story. In the first place, no group of real Oklahomans would go around calling themselves Okies. They were the poor trash who went to California during the Depression and the dust.

"Second place, I checked around. No new Accuseds has bought any sheriffs, including me. And that's the truth.

"Third place, there ain't no motel southwest of Tulsa named The Blue Bell. The closest thing is a scruddy twelve-cabin place called the Blue Moon down in Simpson.

"Fourth place, there's only one guy I know of around in the transportation business who calls himself Boomer. Runs a bus line from Ardmore over to Durant and back. Calls it Boomer Sooner Coaches or something like that. . . .''

"That *is* transportation. The CBS reporter said he was in the transportation business," I said.

"It's just barely transportation, Mack. Boomer owns one bus and a lot of dust. He does the driving himself and all the rest there is to it. It's just barely a business, to tell the truth.''

"Simpson's on the way from Durant to Ardmore," I said, like I was an important detective or somebody who had just figured out something important.

"So?" asked Russell Frank.

"So maybe it all fits."

"Fifth place, Mr. Lieutenant Governor, is for you to forget it. Lieutenant governors should leave going after Accuseds to people like me and C."

I said my good-byes to him and the other regulars in the coffee shop. I knew everybody in there and I knew them well. And I knew most of them still couldn't figure out how and why I ended up lieutenant governor. But they were proud of me and happy for Jackie and that was all that mattered. To them and to me.

I went around the corner to the Continental Trailways bus station.

I had worked there as a ticket agent for a while before I was elected county commissioner. That was when it was Thunderbird Motor Coaches. The Thunderbird, we called it. It ran all through Kansas and Oklahoma before selling out to Continental. The station manager hired me mostly because he was impressed with the way I conducted myself when I went up on the Orpheum stage and swapped talk with Roy, Dale, Gabby and Trigger. But, whatever, I was a super ticket agent. I knew how to make out tickets and read schedule and tariff books and call buses on the PA system better than anybody I ever met or heard of.

I asked the agent at the bus depot if I could see the latest issue of the *Russell's Official National Motor Coach Guide*. He knew who I was and was delighted to be of service to the lieutenant governor of his state. Bus people called the book the Red Guide. It came out every month with all of the bus schedules of every bus company in the country. I stole one once from a bus depot in Lufkin, Texas. Pepper was with me. It was one of the little things I did not tell Arneson and Heket.

There it was on page 508: Boomer Sooner Coaches. Its schedule didn't take up but a few inches down in the left-hand corner, but it was there just like it was Greyhound or Trailways. There were five round trips a day between Durant and Ardmore forty-seven miles away, across Lake Texoma and through Mannsville, Simpson, Madill and Kingston. If Russell Jack was right and Boomer did all the driving himself, he left Ardmore on his first run east at 6:30 in the morning and didn't get back for good until 7:15 that evening.

I decided to catch him in Ardmore. I saw he had a forty-five-minute layover there from 12:15 until he headed back to Durant at 1:00. I had plenty of time to get there and I could even go through Simpson and check out the Blue Moon motel.

No important detective could have planned it better.

But first I had to go by and see Brother Walt.

Going by to see Brother Walt was part of what going to Adabel was always all about. He was the pastor of the First Church of the Holy Road and the man who gave us life when Pepper, Jackie and I came to town. He got me my first job with the county, got Pepper out of jail and into the Marines, presided over Pepper's funeral, married Jackie and me, got me into politics, baptized our children. He was a smart man, a funny man, a great man, a special man, a crazy man, a lovely man, a man I sometimes thought was really Jesus' brother.

Mrs. Ida Henderson, his plump, pleasant, elderly secretary, hugged me as she always did and opened the door for me to go right into Brother Walt's office as she always did.

He was standing out in front of his desk in rubber pants and boots. The pants were held up by suspenders.

Brother Walt was a huge man with a round face and rosy cheeks who always seemed to be smiling.

"Well, God is Great," he said. "If it isn't the beloved lieutenant governor of our beloved state. Meet Mr. Wilkie, Mack."

Mr. Wilkie was sitting in a chair off in the corner of the office. He was a small man in a black suit, white shirt and dark blue tie.

"Mr. Wilkie is a sales representative with our publishing and church equipment house in Fort Worth. The Church of the Holy Road publishing church equipment house," said Brother Walt in that smooth, God's son-like voice of his. "He's trying to sell me this baptistry outfit. Guaranteed to keep me dry as I baptize new souls for Jesus. Guaranteed, is that not right, Mr. Wilkie?"

"Yes, sir," said Mr. Wilkie, who was almost thirty, almost bald and definitely disconcerted about a lieutenant governor having just walked in on his sales appointment.

"God is Great," Brother Walt said. "What do you think, Mack? Does it do anything for me? The old baptistry is leaking. I've got to get either this outfit or a whole new baptistry. Look at that catalogue over there. Mr. Wilkie, let the lieutenant governor of Oklahoma look at your catalogue."

The whole thing was a bit spooky. Brother Walt had suffered a heart attack some fifteen years earlier while baptizing several high school boys. I was there when it happened. And remembered it like it happened yesterday. Any yesterday.

Mr. Wilkie brought his catalogue over to me. He turned it to the Baptismal Boots and Trousers write-up. It said the chest wader, or upper part, was made of double-ply nylon and the boots were extra strong and laminated. The suspenders were adjustable, the buttons noncorrosive and there was an inside pocket for a Bible or other written materials. The price was $55.

Mr. Wilkie then turned to the large colored display advertisement for the New Way Baptistry. There was a color picture of a young man in a white robe sitting inside a big glass-enclosed bathtub-looking thing with an older man in a purple robe standing outside. He had one hand on the young man's shoulder, the other in the air up by his head, palm up. The price was $945, FOB, Fort Worth.

Brother Walt joined us for a look.

"See what it says there are its great features, Mack? 'A. The pastor never goes into the water—he is directly behind the baptistry—completely dry. B. The candidate sits—he feels more secure in the water and the top of his head is in an ideal position for the pastor. C. The toehold helps support the candidate—a fear of the water is minimized as the built-in toehold allows the candidate to use his own strength in helping the pastor raise him from the water. . . .' "

"I'm just passing through," I said. "Got to run."

"How is our crazy governor's plan to put a dome on the capitol coming?"

"Great."

"How is my Jackie of the JackieMarts?"

"Great."

"And the children of the Jackie of the JackieMarts?"

"Great."

"Has Tommy Walt got one over the plate yet?"

"Nice to meet you, Mr. Wilkie," I said.

Brother Walt gave my right hand a crush and I left to pursue my work as an important detective.

I sat there in my car on the north side of the tracks for nearly fifteen minutes while a freight upped and backed and switched and made itself a nuisance to people and motorized traffic in Simpson, Oklahoma. The only problem I ever had with Simpson was the train. There always seemed to be one stopped on the track that ran through the center of town. It happened in Adabel and it happened in Madill and in Pauls Valley and a lot of other places, too, but it always seemed worse in Simpson. As if the people who ran the Burlington Railroad had a special grudge against Simpson, so they fouled up and delayed the traffic there the most.

The Blue Moon Motor Court was just on the other side of the tracks. I could see it through the cracks between rail cars but I couldn't get to it.

But I could see enough to know Russell Jack was right. It was scruddy.

And when the train finally got out of the way and I drove across, I could see it for sure. Those twelve cabins looked like they had not been cleaned, painted or maybe even entered in twenty-five or thirty years.

There was a lady sitting out front on two wooden steps that led up to the first cabin with a foot-long sign over the door that said "Office." A sign that was very barely visible above it said "Blue Moon Motor Court." There was a faded shape of a blue moon with it.

The woman was sixty or more years old, her hair was wrapped up and covered by a dirty pink towel. She was smoking a nonfilter cigarette. It was a long one like a Pall Mall.

"You work here?" I asked when I finally got over there, parked and got out of my car. I was driving my own dark blue Buick four-door, by the way. The state would reimburse my mileage and other expenses. There was talk around of someday providing a state-owned car for the lieutenant governor, but it hadn't happened yet.

"Work is work, pork is pork," she said.

"Do you know Boomer Webster, who owns the bus line?"

"Boomer Sooner, Boomer Sooner," she said, like she was singing the O.U. fight song without the music.

"Did he ever come here and have a big meeting with some other people?"

"How many of there are you?" She gave me a good look.

She had eyes that were so bloodshot you couldn't tell what their real color was. If she ever had to fill out a driver's license or any other kind of form that said "Color Eyes" she would have to put "Blood."

I didn't answer and she said, "Who do you say you are?"

"I say I am the lieutenant governor of Oklahoma."

"You're the first to say that. The others all had other things than that to say they were."

"Like what?"

"Like the FBI or the OBI or *The Daily Oklahoman*, the *World*, the *Journal* or a radio station or a TV network. . . ."

I wasn't the only one who planned like an important detective.

"What did they want to know?"

"Same thing. Was there ever a meeting here?"

"What did you tell them?"

"Same thing I'm telling you."

"Which is what?"

"There has never been a meeting of any kind here."

"Did any of them ask you about Boomer Webster?"

"No. That's new with you."

"Thank you."

Thank God.

The Ardmore bus depot was at the corner of First and Washington, right downtown. The main entrance was on Washington, which ran north and south, and the buses loaded and unloaded along the side on First. There were four saw-toothed docks for the buses, each formed in concrete with curbs. Boomer and his bus were already there when I got there.

His bus was in the last dock. The bus was awful-looking. At one time it had been painted green and yellow, but somebody tried to paint the green part blue and the yellow part orange. But neither took very well. Boomer Webster must have then come along with a paintbrush and tried to turn it red and white in the colors of O.U. The result was a mess, like some kids had been finger-painting all over it. Across the top in lettering that shook and wobbled like the same kids had done it were the two words "Boomer Sooner." I knew a lot about buses, but I did not immediately recognize the make or model. Up close I saw that it was made by Fitzjohn—the Fitzjohn Company of Muskegon, Michigan. It had a snubbed nose and about twenty-five seats. I figured it had to be at least twenty years old. If you didn't know better, you'd expect to buy cotton candy from it instead of riding it to Durant.

Boomer Webster also had a snubbed nose. But the rest of him was huge. Maybe as much as 250 pounds huge. I found him sitting on a counter stool in the bus depot coffee shop eating a cheeseburger with fries, onion rings and a Pepsi. He was wearing black trousers and a gray uniform shirt with no tie and no cap. His hair was thin and red, his face wide and red.

I sat down next to him.

"You Boomer Webster?" I said.

"That's me." He said it cheerfully, pleasantly, like he was delighted to be Boomer Webster. "What can I do for you?"

"That's some bus you have out there," I said like an important detective.

"I'm leaving at one o'clock for Durant if that's where you're headed too."

"No, thanks. I'm going the other way. Driving in my own car. Just stopped in for lunch."

An unpleasant waitress who was short-haired and about fifty took my order. For luck I ordered my all-time favorite meal, a tunafish-salad sandwich and a Grapette.

"No Grapette," she said, like if I wasn't so ignorant I would have already known such an obvious and important thing.

I ordered a Dr Pepper and she went away.

"There's something about people who work in bus station cafés that drives me nuts," Boomer said. "They're used to dealing with people they'll never see again, so they treat everybody like garbage. Sorry about her."

"I'm used to bus station cafés," I said. "Thanks for caring. Didn't you play football at O.U.?" Smooth. Detective on the move.

"Not me."

"You look like a right guard to me."

"Left tackle. But only in high school and one semester at East Central State."

"Got the name Boomer from playing football, I guess?" Casual. Ever so detective casual was I.

"Nope. I left school to go to work in the oil fields outside Enid. They started calling me Boomer there because I could yell loud."

"You ever see any of your old football buddies?"

"Nope. Didn't have any to speak of."

"How long a day do you put in on that bus?"

"Twelve, fourteen. Depends on how she's operating. Seven days a week."

"Must not leave much time for any personal or outside life."

"Nothing much personal or outside going on. Just a wife and three babies."

I got my tunafish-salad sandwich and Dr Pepper and started eating. Boomer was finishing up.

"How did you get in the transportation business?" I asked.

"You mean my bus?"

"You bet."

"I drove a bus for M.K.&O. Lines out of Tulsa and then for Jordan Bus Company out of Hugo for a while, and finally decided to go into business for myself. All it takes is no brains, a banker, a bus and a lot of time."

"How's business?"

"Lousy, but I like working for myself. Wouldn't trade it for nothing."

A young man came up to him on the other side. He was unshaven and poorly dressed and had a strong odor of drink on him. He did not sit down, but he started talking a mile a minute. "Mr. Boomer, it's me again and I have got to go to Durant. I have a dollar and a half to my name but I promised to buy some groceries of some kind today and if I come home without any, that will be the end of it for me. So if you could see your way clear to taking me to Durant I will pay you back. I know I already owe you for another trip or two. But things are changing. I need to get back to Durant."

Boomer was smiling the whole time the man talked. Now he reached over and touched his shoulder. "Go find yourself a seat on the bus. I'll be ready to go in a few minutes."

"Thank you, Mr. Boomer. Thank you very much."

"That kind of thing happen very often?" I asked when the man was gone.

"Sure," said Boomer. "I love it."

"Love it? You can't make any money hauling people for nothing."

"It makes me feel good when I do. So if it makes me feel good, then it doesn't matter. In fact it's better. Taking people on my bus for nothing is about the only way I have to make myself feel good right now. What do you do to make yourself feel good?"

"Nothing like that, I'm sorry to say. Aren't you concerned people will start taking advantage of you? How do you know that man can't afford to pay?"

Boomer laughed. "I can tell if a man is lying about something like that. But it doesn't matter, if it makes me happy. I'm going back and forth between here and Durant five times a day as long as that bus runs. Why not fill up the seats with people any way I can? I've got to go anyhow."

He picked up his check, got up from his seat, put a quarter down as a tip. "Enjoyed talking to you. What do you do?"

"I'm the lieutenant governor of Oklahoma." There was no point in playing important detective anymore.

Boomer smiled and then stopped smiling and looked at me hard. "How did you lose that eye? In a war?"

"No."

He took two steps away and then came back. "You really the lieutenant governor?"

"Yes, sir."

"What in the hell are you doing sitting at this counter in this bus depot talking like this to a regular person?"

"Taking pulses of the people."

"What do you want to know?"

"What do you make of the Okies story? Hard to believe we've got our own Mafia, isn't it?"

Boomer shook his head. "What Okies story? You got me on that kind of stuff. I'm probably not the right person to take any pulses from. I don't pay any attention to what's going on anywhere except on that little bus of mine."

"Well, thanks just the same," I said.

He stuck out his right hand. I took it and shook it. It was a lot like shaking hands with a pillow.

"Better luck with the next pulse you take, sir," he said.

"Thank you, Boomer."

He left and I returned to my lunch.

Fifteen minutes later I was in my car and on Highway 77 headed back to Oklahoma City. I was returning with two rock-solid pieces of information.

A. No sinister crime ring worth its sinister salt would have had an organized meeting at the Blue Moon Motor Court in Simpson, Oklahoma.

B. Boomer Webster, owner and operator of Boomer Sooner Coaches, would not have been there if it did have such a meeting there or anywhere else in the world.

I received two important phone calls at home that evening. The first came during the news.

There had been nothing yet on CBS about the Okies. Most of the top of the newscast was spent on the Watergate story. One of the Washington newspapers had had some kind of story about what Attorney General Mitchell knew, and everybody was denying it. Roger was still substituting for Walter.

Before the first commercial break, Buffalo Joe was on the phone.

"It was just on NBC! It was just on NBC! Heket saw it himself. They had pictures of some ratty place called The Blue Moon in Simpson. What's going on, Mack? What in the name of Texas hell is going on?"

"I don't know. Sheriff Russell Jack Franklin down at Adabel says it's a figment."

"A what? A what?"

"A figment of the imagination. Like C. said. A crock."

"Damn it, Mack, CBS and NBC are not in the figment-and-crock business. C. just doesn't want to admit there was a big organized crime ring here he didn't know about. Heket said the NBC guy said the FBI and Senate crime committees and half of Washington are fighting among themselves about it, too. They're all accusing the others of holding out on the others, holding out on the others."

"Yes, sir."

"Heket and Arneson say, Heket and Arneson say we must depend on you, Mack. We'll have a press conference in the morning and we will tell everybody you're in charge."

"In charge of what? In charge of what?"

"Of the State of Oklahoma's efforts to get to the bottom of this awful plague on our Sooner society."

"Yes, sir. Thank you."

"It's got to be either you or me and I've got a lot of other fish to fry right now. Particularly the dome. Particularly the dome. I will not rest peacefully as long as our capitol building remains domeless. Nobody in Oklahoma should. Nobody in Oklahoma. We must Crown Oklahoma, Mack."

"Crown Oklahoma, Joe."

"Let's get together first thing in the morning to compare notes on what we'll tell the press. Let's get together first thing."

It would be my first press conference.

The second call came much later.

It was several seconds before I realized it was the phone that was ringing. I turned on the light by the bed. The electric alarm clock Jackie gave me for Christmas two years before showed the time as 12:45 A.M. Not since my days as county commissioner in Adabel, when flood waters washed away bridges and roads, had I been awakened in the middle of the night by a ringing phone.

I picked it up, expecting the very worst. Jackie was sitting right in bed with me doing the same.

"Is this the lieutenant governor?" It was a man's voice.

"Yes."

"The one who was at the bus depot in Ardmore today?"

"Yes."

"The one who ordered a tunafish sandwich and a Grapette, and when the waitress said they didn't have Grapettes ordered a Dr Pepper?"

"Yes."

"You really are the lieutenant governor?"

"Yes."

"Well, this is Boomer Webster."

I had about recognized his voice. I was relieved. I smiled and whispered to Jackie that it was nothing to worry about.

"What can I do for you, Boomer?"

"There are strange things going on down here, sir. Very strange. I had seventeen passengers on the last trip east to Durant. Seventeen! There haven't been seventeen people on my little bus at one time ever! Ever! Then there were twenty-one going back west on the next trip. Some of them rode both ways and they and others added up to nineteen on the return. I got out of the bus there in Ardmore after the final run, and there were people around in coats and ties watching me. Scads of them. Some of them followed me to the lot where I park the bus for the night and then on to the house. This was VFW night so I went up there for while, and a bunch of people in cars followed me and waited for me outside. I stopped at the 7-Eleven to get some chocolate milk for my little daughter Mattie, who's five. Two of them even came in and read magazines while I was buying the milk. . . ."

"What did they look like?"

"Like bad bankers. Dark suits, white shirts and striped ties. Had hats on, a dressy kind of hat only people somewhere else wear."

"You been to a lot of movies, Boomer?"

"Not a whole lot, but a lot."

"Did they look like cops or criminals?"

"Both. They were both kinds. Definitely all kinds."

"Did they talk to each other?"

"No. Well, some of them did. But I got the idea some of them were following some of the others as much as me."

"Anybody with cameras or people looking like reporters?"

"I never saw a movie with reporters in it. I don't know what they look like."

"Has anybody said to you they were a reporter and asked you any questions?"

"No, sir."

"Good."

"Why's that good?"

"I'm not sure."

"Look, I'm worried. First there was you at the bus depot and now all of these people. What's going on, Mister Lieutenant Governor?"

"There's nothing to worry about. You are not in danger."

"You sure?"

"I swear on my oath as lieutenant governor of Oklahoma."

"That's good enough for me. Thanks."

"You're welcome. Now go back to bed. You want to be fresh for your 6:30 east in the morning."

"How did you know my first run was 6:30?"

"Saw it in the Red Guide."

"You read the Red Guide?"

"You bet."

"Boy, you really are one smart politician."

"Thank you."

I had much, much trouble going back to sleep.

5

In the Flesh

Buffalo Joe loved press conferences. He loved it when he walked into the room and the reporters got quiet while he said, "Good morning, ladies and gentlemen of the Oklahoma press. Good morning, good morning. First question, first question." That first question always came from the dean of the state capitol press corps, G. G. McMahan of the *Oklahoma City Times*, who also ended it by saying, "Thank you, Governor." Just like at the White House.

Joe loved it when he could make the reporters laugh with him in spite of themselves. When he got off a good clean chop at some opponent. When he effectively dodged a particularly difficult question or subject. But most particularly when just standing there he came up with some brilliant new idea off the top of his head. That's where the idea of doing something about the capitol's dome problem came from. A visiting reporter from Nowata began a question about a new highway signs proposal by saying this was only her second trip to Oklahoma City, and driving in from the north she wasn't sure she was going to find the capitol building because the route was so poorly marked and there was no capitol dome to see from miles away, like there was in every other state capital city in the United States of America. "Someday there will be a dome," Joe said spontaneously. "Someday there will be. Someday there must be. I will see to it. I will see to it." There were a couple of follow-up questions and Joe had spontaneously committed himself to building a dome. It was the main story of the Oklahoma day.

Governor Hayman Proposes Dome for Capitol! Says We've Been Domeless Too Long!

That experience led Joe even more to see press conferences as inspirational opportunities. He tried to hold them as often as he could without appearing to overdo it, which meant at least one every two weeks. He always held them in the big conference room off the main corridor from his office. There was a large table and enough chairs for the twenty or thirty people who usually showed up.

But not so for this one. It was scheduled for the Blue Room, the huge room around another corner and down the hall that was normally used for major receptions and bill signings. They were expecting a large crowd of reporters from all over the state and the nation. The time was set for eleven o'clock.

I went to his office at ten to check in first thing, to find out what he was going to say and what he expected me to say. He was too busy to see me right then. It was a first-time reversal for the Open Mack Policy. I came back a few minutes later. Still busy. His secretary said she would call me when he had a minute.

She never called.

So I walked into the press conference at eleven sharp without even a figment of an idea of what was going to happen.

The Blue Room was jammed. All one hundred or so folding chairs set up in neat rows were taken. The statehouse press corps regulars were all there, but so were seventy-five or eighty other people I had never seen before. Usually there were three, maybe four, television cameras set up. There were fifteen this morning.

Buffalo Joe made his appearance at four minutes after eleven. He came over and shook my hand and whispered, "Crown Oklahoma, Mack. Sorry we couldn't get together beforehand, together beforehand. Had some business on the dome project that just wouldn't wait. A guy in Blackwell's got an idea for getting radio and TV stations to pay for the dome in exchange for putting powerful antennas up there."

We walked to a podium. Lights came on in our faces. Cameras rolled.

"Good morning, ladies and gentlemen of the Oklahoma press," said Buffalo Joe. "To everyone else, an Oklahoma welcome to the capitol. Those of you from out of state, welcome to our Sooner State of Oklahoma. We are always delighted to see people here from other states. Oklahoma's a lot like the chocolate fudge, like the chocolate fudge all of our mothers used to make. It sticks to your fingers and to your heart and soul. Oklahoma is made up of people who came here to find their way and their futures. . . ."

"Governor!" some ill-mannered reporter yelled. "What about the Okies?" I didn't know the person, of course. No Oklahoman would be so rude.

Joe kept talking.

"But we are all here this morning to do other business. We know many of you have traveled from afar to probe the story going around about an alleged organized crime group with Oklahoma origins. It is a plague on our Sooner society and we are delighted this morning to say we are hard at work to rid it from the face of our fertile Oklahoma earth. Our effort is under the direction of our esteemed lieutenant governor. He is here with us now to give you a progress report.''

He turned to me and then back to the reporters and said: "Again, welcome to the state capitol of Oklahoma. Welcome to the state capitol of Oklahoma. If any of you would like to contribute to our fund to build a dome on the top of this building, feel free to do so before leaving. All contributions are tax deductible and would be most appreciated. I would also suggest our dome dream to you as the real story going on in Oklahoma right now. It is the real story of Oklahoma. Bye for now.''

He waved and walked out of the room!

That left me standing there by myself with cameras and microphones and pencils running.

Some of the reporters yelled questions and other things at him, but he just kept walking.

The room got quiet again. The reporters assumed I had a statement and waited for me to start talking.

I cleared my throat a time or two. Then said:

"I, too, would like to welcome all of you to this news conference and to Oklahoma. As the governor said, we are trying our best to get to the bottom of this Okies business. But I have nothing concrete to report at this time. You might be better served putting your questions to some of your fellow reporters. Clearly there is one or maybe more who know much about what is going on, but do not think it their duty as citizens to tell the duly constituted officials of government. They obviously feel a two-minute report on television is more important to the common good than actually putting alleged perpetrators of serious crimes behind bars. Maybe they will tell *you* what they know. They have thus far refused to tell us. We join with the rest of America every night to find out the next chapter in this spectacular story about crime and criminals. It is with regret that I say both the crimes and the criminals could be easily stopped if the persons with the information about them wanted it so. Thank you.''

I started for the same door Joe went through.

''Hey! Wait a minute!'' somebody yelled. And then there was a chorus of screamed questions.

''Have you found them?'' ''Did you know about it before?'' ''Have you made any arrests?'' ''Details. We want details.'' ''Are you talking about CBS?''

Several of the reporters blocked my way out. One of them, an older man who dressed and talked like he was from Illinois or New York or some such place, screamed at me: ''We demand more information!'' A younger man with no tie on said, ''Do you deny you can't break them?''

Deny we can't break them?

My eye caught a man standing in the back of the room who was not rushing to me or anywhere else. He had his hands in his pockets and he was smiling like he was king of the mountain.

It was Archibald Tyler, CBS News, Washington, in the flesh. In the awful snaky flesh. He looked as puffy in person as he did on television. I wanted to go over to him and say: Okay, did you hear me just now? What's your answer? Are you a reporter or are you a citizen? What else do you know? Tell us, so we can do something about it. C. says it's a crock anyhow. Sheriff Russell Jack Franklin of Adabel says it's a figment. There's no Blue Bell motel south of Tulsa. The only thing even close is the Blue Moon Motor Court in Simpson, and nothing ever happened there. Boomer Webster is no crime boss and no other Boomer candidates have surfaced. What do you say about all of that? Why are you picking on Oklahoma? Go back to Washington and tell us all about who broke into that Watergate apartment or whatever. Leave us alone.

The other reporters finally let me out the door. A TV guy I did not recognize said, just as I stepped out in the hall: "Well, at least will you tell us how you lost your eye?"

I said quietly, firmly, magnificently: "Stan Musial knocked it out with a hard liner down the third-base line."

"You played major-league ball? When? For whom? What position? . . ."

It wasn't the first harmless little lie I had ever told in my life. But it was the first to a reporter since becoming lieutenant governor of Oklahoma. And it felt good.

It felt good.

There was a visitor waiting for me back at my office. C., the one-eared director of the Oklahoma Bureau of Investigation, had come to see the one-eyed lieutenant governor. Two of his young agents were not with him. He was upset.

"The Chip refused to see me," he said, like his words were spit. "His secretary said to see you."

"Well, you're seeing me," I said.

C. was standing when I came in and I did not sit down. I guess it was my way of letting him know I didn't have a whole lot of time to chat with him, either. Two can play.

"This is a crazy business, Mack," he said. Mack? "My people tell me there are Mafia hoods, FBI agents, Senate crime committee investigators, reporters from every rag in the Western world and all other kinds of worthless unsavories crawling over southeastern Oklahoma like red fire ants on a hill of sugar."

"I know. I was there yesterday."

"You were?"

"Yes."

"My people say they're really swarming around some poor bus guy in Ardmore. . . ."

"Name is Boomer Webster. He's clean. I talked to him myself."

"Yeah, he's clean. Everybody's clean. There is no such thing as the Okies, I'm telling you."

"It's a figment?"

"Yeah. A crock."

"Russell Jack Franklin down in Adabel agrees with you."

His eyes narrowed even narrower than they already were, which was narrow enough. "Russell Jack a friend of yours?"

"Yes. We worked for the same county government. I know how he operates, but I am not part of it, if that's what you're wondering. I am not now nor have I ever been on the take, C. Relax."

C.

His eyes went back to their normal width. "Nobody's ever been able to pin anything on Russell Jack. We've tried and so have the feds," he said. "All of that aside, he knows his business. If he says it's a figment, then you should listen."

"The governor says CBS, NBC and all the rest don't put figments and crocks on the news."

"Well, you tell The Chip they have this time."

We looked at each other a couple of seconds and then I walked over to my desk and picked up a piece of paper like it was important and I had to get right on it.

"I'm around if you need me," said C. "It's my job. It's a job for law enforcement to clean this thing up, not for . . . well . . ."

"Politicians?"

"Precisely."

He started to go. I stopped him with a hand signal.

"Have you run checks on Blue Bell motels just to see if it's more than a crock?" I asked in my most lieutenant governor manner.

"There are five in the state. None southwest of Tulsa. Two of them, both up in the Panhandle, are out of business. One in Tonkawa is run by two Methodist preachers' widows. One in Vinita hasn't had more than five customers on one night in twenty years. One over at Bethany is now a Best Western. We interviewed everybody who works and ever has worked there. Nothing. We also ran checks on all O.U. football teams going back to nineteen forty-five. Are there any of them who still hang around together as a group? Are there any with guys who have been in trouble with the law? Are there any with guys named Boomer on them? Nothing. We also checked out everybody in this state with a record whose nickname is Boomer. There aren't any. We also checked and double-checked to see if there is even a smell of organized crime activity anywhere anyplace. We asked the FBI and we had some friends in Washington check with the Senate Organized Crime Select Committee. Nothing. They're all as mystified as we are. We asked every police force, every sheriff's office, to talk to every informer they know. Nothing. We sent word to McAlester and had our snitches check to see if anyone in prison knew anything about anything. Nothing. We're clean. The State of Oklahoma is clean. It's a crock."

He gave me a little salute like he was about to leave my ship. "You have my number, Mack." And away he went.

I assumed Archibald Tyler, CBS News, Washington, was staying at the most expensive hotel in Oklahoma City. I assumed correctly. He was at the Park Plaza downtown. It was the middle of the day so I did not expect to find him in, but I asked the operator to ring his room anyhow.

"Hello," said the now familiar squeaky voice.

"I would like to talk to you, Mr. Tyler," I said to him after identifying myself.

"I heard your little sermon at the press conference. Was that me you were referring to?"

"Good guess. I would like to talk to you now, Mr. Tyler."

"You want to interview me, or do you want me to interview you?"

"I just want to talk. This is a very serious matter. As you know, people have already been killed because of your stories."

"Mafia hit men hitting other Mafia hit men is not people getting killed. It's a public service."

"Please cooperate with us."

"Mudd told me about your call to him. Sorry. Can't help you either."

"You won't even talk to me?"

There was a count of five—maybe six or seven—before he said, "No."

"No? I don't get it. . . ."

"I'm busy right now. I'm working on another story for tonight."

"What story?"

"Watch the *CBS Evening News* with Roger Mudd Substituting for the Vacationing Walter Cronkite," he squeaked. "You're in it yourself. A sound bite from your news conference. I do have one question for you, come to think of it. Somebody said you played major-league baseball with the Cleveland Indians. Is that right?"

They couldn't even get my lie straight. Wrong league, among other things.

"No comment," I said. And hung up.

* * *

Dad called from Hutchinson.

"Hey, Lieutenant Governor Son, everybody around here's talking about the Okies," he said. "Sergeant Johnny Staley from Dodge City—I don't think you know him—called a while ago to say thank God they aren't from Kansas or they'd be called the Sunflowers. Hardly a real swanky name for a crime ring."

Cool it with the jokes, okay, Dad, I wanted to say. But didn't.

He said nobody at the KBI or anywhere else had ever heard a thing about the Okies. "You sure they're for real?"

"CBS is," I said.

"Well, then let CBS catch 'em and hang 'em."

"That's already what's happening, whether we like it or not."

"Don't let it upset you like this, son."

"Hard not to be upset when the whole world is being told about an Oklahoma Mafia that we can't even find, much less catch and prosecute."

"The important thing is to stay busy," he said. "Sit on your behind and wait, and your investigation sits on *its* behind and waits. Do something. Anything. But do something. Keep the trails hot."

"Thanks, Dad."

He asked about Tommy Walt's pitching and I lied and said he was doing fine. "Are you sure he shouldn't have stayed in the infield?" Dad asked.

"He could not catch a fly ball. He could not hit a curve. There was nothing else for him to do but pitch. We have been through all of that a hundred times." My tone was sharp and testy.

"Sorry. Good luck with finding the Okies," he said.

"If you do find them, send them packing south across the Red River to Texas, not up this way to Kansas."

"Yes, sir."

"No 'yes, sir' necessary, son. Just a joke. Give my love to Jackie and the kids."

We hung up. I felt bad but not enough to call him back and apologize.

Stay busy. Keep the trails hot. Great advice, Lieutenant Dad.

I had only two full-time staff members, a legislative assistant and an administrative assistant/secretary. The legislative assistant, who brought in several part-timers to help out when the legislature was in session, was a young up-and-comer recent O.U. law school graduate named Douglas Vermillion. He was away on vacation, so he could not help me run down the Okies. That left only Janice. Janice Alice Montgomery. She was a nice lady from Cordell who had only one bad habit. She called everybody Dove. I heard she did the same thing all thirty years she worked as a secretary in the governor's legislative affairs office, before she was promoted to be administrative assistant to the lieutenant governor. She answered the phone and typed up what few letters and other things I had to do. There wasn't that much, so I had no complaints and neither did she.

I called her in and instructed her to clip every story about the Okies from every newspaper she could find. And not just those from Oklahoma. I gave her ten dollars and told her to go to the library or a hotel newsstand somewhere and find copies of newspapers from New York, Washington, Kansas City, Los Angeles and other places. And to pick up *Time* and *Newsweek* and *U.S. News and World Report*.

I asked if she had friends who watched television. She said all of her friends did mostly that every night. I asked her to sit down with them and see if she could find out if they remembered how many stories about the Okies they had seen on the other networks besides CBS. The same for anybody who might have heard about it on the radio.

"I'll go right to work on this, Dove," she said.

I was suddenly in no mood to be called Dove anymore. So I said, "Why do you call people that?"

"What?"

"Dove."

"It's a habit I picked up from my father when I was nine years old."

Janice Alice Montgomery was now in her late sixties. She was short and thin like a car radio aerial. Her hair was also short. And dyed black like coal.

"People just do not go around calling people the names of birds," I said. My tone, I regret to say, was just like it was with Dad—short and testy.

"My father did and so do I. So there are two people who do or did. You want me to stop calling you Dove? Is that it?"

There were tears in her eyes. They were dark brown.

"I'd like that, yes, please. It just doesn't sound right."

"It sounded all right to six governors and seven lieutenant governors before you."

"I'm sorry."

"It has sounded all right to four different United States senators from Oklahoma and maybe fifty different congressmen, including Speaker Carl Albert. To no telling how many members of the Oklahoma House and the Senate and state treasurers and auditors and other officials. I have been calling people Dove for an awful lot of years now. An awful lot. You alone are the only one in all of those years who ever suggested that I not call them Dove. Don't you find that stimulating?"

Stimulating? I made the decision not to answer that question.

"The dove is a beautiful bird," she said. "It's the bird of peace, you know." And she left my office.

I took out a yellow legal-sized pad and wrote "To Do" at the top. Then I wrote "A" on the top left-hand side.

And I sat there thinking. For a long time.

Finally I wrote: "Watch tonight's *CBS Evening News*."

I couldn't think of anything else.

I called Jackie at JackieMart–Eastside to tell her I was going to stay at the office to watch the news and attend to business. She said she would see me at home later.

"There was a man from Boise City in here today. He said he was prepared to put together a financing package to bring JackieMarts to the Panhandle. How about that?"

"Great news. Really great news."

"Found the Okies yet?" she said.

"No."

"None came into any of our stores today. If one does I'll tell them to report directly to you and Buffalo Joe at the capitol."

"Hush, Dove."

"Dove?"

Archibald Tyler's report was from in front of our beloved state capitol building. He stood on the south side just to the left of *Cowboy on a Wild Pony*, a glorious bronze statue of a wild horse with his rider, rearing up because of a prickly pear on the trail. It was the work of Constance Whitney Warren and was supposed to be dedicated by Will Rogers in 1930, but he couldn't make it and nobody else got around to it until 1957.

Tyler's squeaked-out words were like hot shots to my heart, stomach and brain.

"There is bedlam in the government of the State of Oklahoma over the story of the Okies, the new organized crime setup that is Oklahoma based and manned. It was clear from the performances of the governor and the lieutenant governor today that they were caught by surprise, that they knew nothing of the Okies before the group was publicly exposed by CBS News."

There were pictures of Buffalo Joe and me at the press conference. And then it switched to just me, and the whole world heard and saw me say: "We are trying our best to get to the bottom of this. But we have nothing concrete to report at this time." They cut it off before I said the stuff about asking reporters to help us put these criminals in jail. Of course.

Tyler kept talking while the picture showed me trying to get out of the room.

What he said was just awful:

"While state authorities are having trouble finding out what's going on, CBS News learned further details of the Okies' operations. Reliable sources told us the Okies operate mostly from large cars and trucks with two-way radios. They said the bulk of their crimes are committed outside of the State of Oklahoma, which is used by them mostly as a safe haven. Law enforcement authorities in the state have never bothered them because they do their dirty work elsewhere.

"We also learned today that squads of FBI and Internal Revenue Service agents and investigators of the Senate Organized Crime Task Force have flocked to Oklahoma to pursue their separate probes. There have already been complaints of failure to coordinate and cooperate.

"Local news organizations here are reporting an additional influx of well-dressed men, who they say have an appearance of being connected to organized crime families in the East. CBS could not independently confirm these reports.

"Meanwhile, the governor of Oklahoma urged news reporters to report on another story."

The camera zoomed from Tyler and *Cowboy on a Wild Pony* upward and backward to the domeless top of the capitol.

"It's about a new drive to finally put a dome atop the state capitol building. There was supposed to be one up there, but they ran out of money when the building was erected in nineteen fifteen. The governor says that is the real story of Oklahoma, not the one about an organized crime organization they can't find. . . . Archibald Tyler, CBS News, Oklahoma City."

I went around to the house phones next to the front desk and asked the operator to ring the room of Archibald Tyler, CBS News, Oklahoma City. There was no answer. The desk clerk gave me a message form and I wrote on it: "Mr. Tyler: I must talk to you. Please call me at 555-8910 tonight. Or at my office tomorrow at 555-9146. It is urgent. Thank you."

The room clerk took it and I headed for the door. The Park Plaza was one fancy hotel. As best I could tell, everything in it was either gold or silver, just like its guests. I had never stayed there, but I had gone to several important receptions and other events in its meeting rooms and ballrooms. Buffalo Joe's inaugural ball was the biggest. He instructed me to dance with the wives of as many members of the legislature as I could but not do it so close that our bodies touched. I told him I did not dance, close or far, with women who were not my wife. It made me nervous.

"Nervous you might do something forward, do something forward?" he asked. Like he had just heard I was an uncontrollable sex maniac and that he was about to lose another Second Man of Oklahoma.

"Nervous that I don't dance well enough to stay off their fancy shoes and toes," I replied.

Just as I got to the outside door, it occurred to me Tyler could be in the hotel restaurant.

Important Detective strikes again.

"Good evening," I said to him as I came up to his table. He was sitting alone back in a corner. I admired and envied people who could be comfortable eating alone in restaurants. I hated it and did everything I could to avoid it. Tyler had a steak and a baked potato half eaten and a whole bottle of red wine almost half drunk. The steak was as red in the middle as the wine. Stupid way to eat good meat, in my opinion. It should be cooked clear through so you can chew it. Otherwise, forget it. Cook it so you can't hear the moo, is what they say in southeastern Oklahoma. I'm with them.

Tyler was clearly not happy to see me. But he did squeak out a tiny grin.

"May I join you for a minute?" I did not wait for an answer. I sat down.

"I have no statement to make," he said. And he laughed. He must have thought the idea of a reporter refusing to make a statement to a public official was hilarious.

"Did you see my story tonight?" he asked.

"Yes, sir, I did. It made me sick."

"Sick? Come now, Mr. Lieutenant Governor, it's only a story. I thought that was a good shot of you."

"It's the reputation of our state that is at stake here. Your stories are hurting us all over America. Your cuteness there at the end was particularly hurtful—and unnecessary."

"Sorry. Sometimes the truth hurts."

"Let's talk about the truth. . . ."

"I told you. No statements."

"I just want you to tell me where you are getting your information. . . ."

"That's impossible and you know it. Reporters do not talk about their sources."

"All right, tell me, please, who the leaders are, where they are, so we can arrest them and put them out of business. It is your duty as an American to do so."

"I have no such duty to report to you. My duty is to report to the American people. The fact that I have better sources than you do is what we call in Kansas a nasty break."

"Kansas? You from Kansas?"

"Originally, yes, sir. I'm a Jayhawking Sunflower and proud of it."

I made the sudden Important Detective decision not to tell him I, too, was from Kansas.

"Where in Kansas?" was all I said.

"Coffeyville, down in the southeast corner."

"Oh, yeah," I said. "Just over the border from us— from Oklahoma." One of my grandmothers lived in Coffeyville. I had been there so many times I could name half the streets by heart. My favorites were all the streets named for trees. There was one after another running north and south through town. Beginning with Beech on the east to Pine on the west, with Spruce, Willow, Elm, Maple, Walnut, Sycamore and Cedar in between.

Most people from Kansas were regular and easy to like. I did not know what had gotten into Tyler. He was not like any Jayhawking Sunflower I had ever known. Maybe it was appearing on television. Maybe it had turned him into something different from a regular Kansas boy. He had a self-importance about him that I had not seen before in anybody but preachers and politicians. Like he mattered to the world. Like everybody was watching him eat his steak. Like he was a special soul on this earth. We politicians are that way because we get it in our heads we are talking for The People. Preachers are that way because they think they're speaking for God. But where does a TV reporter get his?

I decided in a few minutes that beneath all that non-Kansasness and his puffiness, Archibald Tyler, CBS News, Oklahoma City, was a wreck. I had a feeling that if I said boo, he would come rising out of his chair like a gusher of oil. The man was a sack of nerves. And my sitting there was making it ever, ever so much worse.

Good.

"Where is it written down that reporters don't have the duties of other citizens to assist in the enforcement of the laws of this land?" I said in a parting shot.

"It's written down in something called the Constitution of the United States. It's in the First Amendment."

"I'll check it out of the library and read it. Thank you."

I stood up. We did not shake hands. We did not say another word. I just walked away.

I walked away with the strange feeling that I now knew more than I knew I knew about Archibald Tyler, CBS News, Oklahoma City.

I went back to the office and made two calls. The first was to C. It was after seven o'clock, but he was still at his office at the OBI. I assumed he would be. I don't know why, I just did. He struck me as a man who worked late. Particularly when there was something like an Okies thing going on to work late about.

"You said to call if I needed anything," I said. "Well, here I am. I need more help."

"What is your pleasure?" I read delight in his voice.

I told him I wanted to find out where Archibald Tyler goes and who he talks to, from this minute until he steps on a plane and leaves the State of Oklahoma. Whenever that is.

"You want him tailed?"

"Right."

"You also want his phone tapped?" C. was talking like he was routinely asking me for the time of day.

"Can you do that?"

"The man's in a hotel, right?"

"Right."

"The answer is, Yes, we can do that."

"Would the hotel have records of calls he's made since he got here?"

"Now you are catching on, Mack. Yes. And of those he's received."

"I'd like all of that."

"It's yours."

"When?"

"The tap and the tail will both be on in two minutes. The other information by tomorrow evening. Maybe sooner."

"Boomer Sooner."

"Precisely."

"Is any of this legal?"

"That is not the question. The question is: Is it necessary?"

"I think it is. But tell your people to be careful. If it

got out that we were spying on a national reporter, it would not do any of us any good."

"Are you telling The Chip?"

"No."

"Good. The man's got a big mouth and he'll tell everybody twice."

"I'm not telling him, in order to protect him."

"Precisely."

The second call was to Dad. I asked him to find out everything he could about Archibald Tyler's growing up and background in Coffeyville and Kansas. I told him to be careful, because it would be difficult if it ever got out that a lieutenant in the Kansas State Highway Patrol was investigating a national television reporter.

"It'll get out," he said. "Maybe not tomorrow or next year. Maybe not until both of us are dead, gone and buried. But it'll get out. Everything gets out, son. Everything. Just yesterday I told Billy Boyd, a sergeant at headquarters in Topeka, a top-secret story about J. T. Baker, the major in charge of administration. He's got a girlfriend out here in a town north of Hutch. They've been fooling around since he was a young trooper years ago. I know Billy and I told him to keep it a secret. It wasn't forty-five minutes later that I was on the phone with old Mark B. Southern in the records office. He told me he had just heard that Major Baker had knocked up some girl in Hutch."

"It's not the same thing, Dad."

"Sorry, Lieutenant Governor Son, but you are dead wrong. A secret stops being a secret the second two people know it. Remember that, if you wish to continue to rise to the top of the bottle in the politics of Oklahoma or anywhere else."

"I'm sorry I was a little unpleasant on the phone the last time, Dad," I said.

"There's a lot of strain connected with being lieutenant governor of a state, son. No need to apologize."

"Thanks, Lieutenant Dad."

6

Whopper with Everything

I skipped breakfast and most conversation and went right to the office the next morning.

Janice Alice was already there. She said, "Good morning" instead of, "Good morning, Dove," and handed me a thick file. It had copies of Okies stories from fifteen newspapers. She had gone into the capitol press room and compiled all of the AP and UPI wire stories about them. She had also typed up reports of her conversations with her apartment and nearby retirement home and church friends and acquaintances about what had been seen and heard on radio and television. She had done a good job.

I read and reread it all many times. The most striking thing about the stories was that they were pretty much the same. Almost exactly. Most were based entirely on the reports of Archibald Tyler, CBS News, Oklahoma City. Nobody had any new or different specific facts about the Okies. What they added were quotations from members of Congress, law enforcement officials and others who mostly said somebody had to get to the bottom of it all and clean out this new scourge on America. A senator from New Jersey or some such place said this new organized crime menace had "come from Oklahoma like a flock of beetles carrying the plague." He had an Italian name.

In the middle of my reading, Janice Alice came in with more news that her informants had picked up on morning radio and TV. Bad news.

Four national conventions set to come to Tulsa or Oklahoma City the next year were reported on the verge of canceling. They did not cite the Okies stories as the reason, but that was the insinuation. She said one of her friends called to say she just heard on Mutual Radio that a dinner-theater production of *Oklahoma!* outside Lowell, Massachusetts, was booed by the audience when they broke into the finale, "Oklahoma!" And the worst news of all: A Norman radio station said there was already concern that the O.U. football team and band, both in summer workouts, would be booed when they took the field for the new season in September. "We'll just boo back," Janice Alice quoted some girl French horn player saying.

What I was waiting for were the reports from Dad and C. on Tyler. By noon neither had come. There was nothing else to do so I kept a lunch appointment with a young Oklahoma City architect Buffalo Joe had asked to "coordinate minds and thoughts" about the dome. His name was Wayne Al Meyer. He was about thirty years old and was originally from Duncan. He wanted to talk to me about the problems he was having coordinating the minds and thoughts. He was having trouble weighing legitimate architectural possibilities with legitimate political probabilities and he wanted me to help him. I listened, but that was all. I wasn't about to say a telescope in the dome from O.U.'s department of astrology was better than one from O. State. Or say to forget the idea of a revolving restaurant. Or say Buffalo Joe would be embarrassed at the suggestion the dome be named the Governor Ralph Joseph Hayman Dome. Or say the materials in the construction had to be all native Oklahoman. The only thing I did say was that he was on the right track in advising Joe that an honest-to-God dome expert be hired to consult with us on what to do. I told him I was stunned to learn there was such a thing as a dome expert, but if there was, let's by all means bring him in. Oklahoma had waited nearly sixty years to put up a dome and it would be a shame to blow it now. I liked Wayne Al. I put our lunch on my state expense account. The state auditor was under instructions to approve without question all dome expenditures. Crown Oklahoma.

We went to Bryan's Steak House on North Broadway. I had the sirloin platter with the steak cooked well done, and french fries and cole slaw on the side. And I drank two big glasses of ice tea. Iced tea just goes with a steak. I skipped dessert. I don't remember what Wayne had.

Dad had called while I was out. I returned the call immediately. And Dad got down to business immediately.

"Here's what I've got: Tyler was born in Sedan, west of Coffeyville. His daddy was a pharmacist, mostly at Rexalls. From Sedan they moved all around over there in the southern and eastern part of the state. To Severy, to Olpe, to Altoona, to Cherryvale, to Chetopa, to Humboldt, to Independence and finally to Coffeyville. Tyler was pretty close to being Jack Armstrong, your all-American boy. Straight A's, captain of the football and baseball teams, president of the student body, editor of the paper. You know the type."

Yeah, I knew the type all right. The type I was not. Except for the baseball part. I did play baseball as hard as anybody has, even if I couldn't hit. Particularly curves.

"What position did he play?" I asked Dad.

"In what?"

"Baseball."

"Who knows, who cares? He went on to K.U. at Lawrence and majored in journalism. Editor of the paper. Good grades. First job was with *The Topeka Capital-Journal* as a reporter. Then went on to local television in Kansas City and then CBS hired him and brought him to Washington. He went to law school at night and was assigned to cover the Justice Department. No criminal record. No criminal record for any of his close relatives. No credit problems. No bank problems. Married a girl he met at K.U. She was from Atchison. They had three kids. Divorced a few months ago . . .''

"Divorced?" I said it like he had just said, "Double ax murderer," and Dad picked up on it.

"Being divorced isn't a crime, son." He took a couple of breaths and said, "This guy's gotten to you, hasn't he?"

"He's gotten to the whole state of Oklahoma. Was he ever caught cheating or anything like that in school?"

"Not that shows up."

"Would you mind rechecking that?"

"Forget it, Lieutenant Governor Son. Forget it. There's nothing there. Nothing. He's Jack Armstrong."

"Yes, sir."

"When does Tommy Walt start again?"

"I don't know. The boy's having his problems. Hates pitching, hates putting baggage checks on suitcases."

"Try him in the outfield."

"Too late for that. Can't hit well enough for that anyhow."

"Has he thought about a career in law enforcement?"

"No. He's too short. Look, back to Tyler. Was there anything in there about his tin voice being a problem when he was young?"

"All boys' voices sound like tin when they're young, son."

"But his still does."

"I know. Who cares?"

C. didn't call until after five o'clock. He said he had information for me. Lots of it. Including some dynamite. Why didn't he come by in a car and pick me up? We could talk while we drove. Drove where? Maybe to get a bite, he said.

Five minutes later, I was standing at the basement entrance on the west side of the capitol. C.'s famous unmarked black Lincoln Continental OBI command car arrived. I slid into the backseat next to him. He sat on the right and I was on the left, so my good eye and his good ear matched. The two young men were in the front, one driving, the other riding what C. called "shotgun." Somehow the idea of a group of thugs driving alongside and attempting a shotgun ambush didn't quite ring the bell. But it was fun to think about, fun to be with Oklahoma's chief law enforcement officer, fun to be with a legend in his legendary car.

There was a submachine gun strapped to the back of the front seat on his side of the car. There were also rifles, pistols, gas masks, teargas canisters, bulletproof vests and a wide assortment of flashlights and other paraphernalia tacked on the ceiling and elsewhere for quick and ready use in case of a wide assortment of emergencies.

"You prefer Burger King or McDonald's?" he said after a minute or two.

"I'm a Whopper fan, thank you," I replied.

"Burger King, please, Smitty," he said to the driver, OBI agent Michael M. Smith.

Smitty gunned it up Lincoln Boulevard past The Flamingo, The Palomino, The Trade Winds, The Hacienda Holiday and several other motels on Motel Row to a Burger King. We headed to the drive-thru lane and stopped at the orders speaker.

"It was smart of your wife to think of doing this kind of thing for groceries," C. said. "Nobody likes to get out of the car just to pick up some bread, some milk and a can of beans." I thanked him on behalf of the founder of JackieMarts.

Smitty asked C. and me what we wanted and he did the ordering for us. I had a Whopper with Everything and an order of fries and a large Dr Pepper. C. had a Whopper with Everything but Cheese and a glass of milk. Smith and James ordered nothing for themselves. They've already eaten, C. explained. James was Bob James, the OBI agent riding shotgun.

We drove around to the pick-up window. C. leaned forward and handed Smitty a twenty-dollar bill.

"It's on me, C.," I said.

"It's on the people," said C. I noticed Smitty was careful to get a receipt with the change. The state auditor's office would be pleased. I wondered how I would look on the expense form. "Lieutenant Governor— Whopper with Everything, Fries and Large Dr Pepper."

Smitty drove—cruised—at a slow speed while C. and I ate our supper. We drove out on north to 63rd Street and then west and up on Grand Boulevard through Nichols Hills, Oklahoma City's fanciest neighborhood. We came out on the other end at May Avenue and turned south.

After several solid bites of Whopper and hefty gulps of milk, C. got down to business.

"First, on who Tyler's been talking to. The answer is nobody. At least from the hotel. Only calls going in or out were from CBS producers, cameramen here. Or with the CBS office in Washington. No others. None. What he said to everybody today was technical, mechanical stuff. Meet me here to shoot that picture, there to shoot this or that. Deadlines and the like. He told his assignment editor in Washington late this afternoon he would not have a story tonight. But would probably have something for tomorrow . . ."

"Did he say what the story was?"

"Nope. And the guy in Washington didn't ask. According to the hotel people—bellhops, clerks, doormen and maids—he's barely left his room. And nobody's been up to see him. Best we can tell, the only times he has left the hotel was to go to that press thing you and The Chip had yesterday and to stand up with a microphone in his hand in front of our capitol building.

"He's received no mail, notes, messages. And he's sent none out, at least through the hotel."

He took another couple of bites and swallows of his Burger King supper.

"Well, you were right," I said. "That is real dynamite, all right."

He looked at me like I was a ninny. "I haven't told you the dynamite yet," he said.

C. ate some more of his burger and drank some more of his milk. He swallowed and he wiped his mouth and he got ready. I glanced out the window. The state fairgrounds were coming up on the right. Off in the distance I could barely see the airplanes stuck up on the top of metal poles forty feet or so off the ground. There were four of them there to commemorate aviation's role in Oklahoma progress. There were B-52 and B-47 bombers, a C-47 transport and a small executive business plane used by an oil company.

"The man's a pervert, Mack," said C., in a voice that was low and businesslike.

"A sex kind?"

"What other kinds are there?"

"How do you know he's one?"

"He carries a compact."

"A compact? Like women use to fix their faces?"

"That's exactly the kind of compact I mean. He carries it with him. The hotel maid said she sees it there on the dresser drawers in the room when he is there. A room service waiter testified the same."

"What does it mean then?"

"Well, let's think it through together out loud. Do you know of any men who go around making up their faces like girls?"

"No."

"What would you think about somebody you found that did?"

"I get you, C. I get you."

"You know what I think? I think he stays in that room all day and makes himself up and plays like he's a girl. That's what I think."

"Could be. What do we do about it?"

"We get the word to him that he closes down his reporting about this Okies crock or we'll arrest him for sodomy, which is a thirty-years-to-life felony in this state."

"Sodomy? Carrying a compact is not sodomy, C."

"Let him explain that to an Oklahoma judge."

We had turned back to the east now and were cruising down Reno Avenue toward downtown. Reno was one of my favorite streets because there was a junky bus-repair shop on it that had a late 1940s model Flxible Clipper on its back lot. The Clipper was my favorite bus of all time. The one on the lot was in terrible shape, but its trademark rear air scoop that resembled an upside-down comma was intact. So were its slanted passenger windows. I pointed to it and identified it as a Flxible Clipper to C. as we drove by. He didn't care but he seemed interested in the strange fact that I did. He said he knew a lot of people who liked to look at old cars or trains, but nobody until now who felt the same way about buses.

"I'm not sure threatening him with exposure is the way to go," I said, finally responding to C.'s proposal about Tyler. "If we were wrong, look at the story he'd have. 'Oklahoma Officials, Unable to Find Crime Gang, Threaten Reporter with Smear.' "

"If the smear's right, it's not a smear and there's no story."

The car had stopped. We had gone on through the southern edge of downtown and turned back north on Lincoln Boulevard. The circle was now complete. We were back in the parking lot on the west side of the state capitol building. There was my Buick parked in the spot marked "Lieutenant Governor" in black letters on a white wooden post.

"I'll sleep on it," I said.

I thanked C. for his information, his suggestions and the Burger King supper, and promised to touch base with him tomorrow.

The black Lincoln Continental command car disappeared and I drove out of the lot toward home.

I had asked Janice Alice to have her friends carefully monitor the early evening news programs because of my travels with C. I called her at home to see if NBC or ABC had anything important or new about the Okies. Nothing. But later I decided to watch a ten-o'clock local news program. I was not as religious about watching them as I was the network broadcasts because Jackie and I were sometimes already asleep by then. But the Okies story had changed everything about my TV duties.

I turned on the set to Channel 10, KOCY. The news was the same on all three of our stations every night, but I liked Channel 10 because of the newscasters. Particularly Rusty Boggs, who did their sports. Rusty was from Chickasha. He played pro baseball for five years including part of a season for the Philadelphia Phillies. He was a first baseman power hitter with a serious strikeout tendency. I got to know him personally when he came to Adabel to manage our Adabel Dodgers in the Class C Sooner State League. He talked about baseball a lot better than he played or managed it, and eventually he went on the radio in Adabel. Then they brought him up to Oklahoma City, first on radio and now on TV.

There were stories on the O.U. band and football teams and the convention cancellations. There was also an interview with one of our U.S. senators from Oklahoma promising to goose the FBI and others to get to the root of the whole thing. Buffalo Joe was mentioned only in passing, in a report from Enid about a neon sign company executive's suggestion that the new capitol dome have a flashing neon sign around it saying "Oklahoma Is Number One," in big red letters. So it could be seen in all four directions across to all neighboring states. Particularly across to Texas to the south and Kansas to the north. Then came reports on a couple of auto accidents and a shooting and a dispute over a zoning change in north Oklahoma City.

The stories were read and introduced by the two anchors named Rose and Dave. Rose Washington, a young black woman, and Dave Anderson, a young white man. I suddenly saw something important as I watched them. The TV was on a stand down off the right of the foot of the bed. I jumped out of bed and got down and looked closer.

"What's wrong?" Jackie said, sitting upright in bed. I motioned for her to join me. She did.

"Look," I said. "Look closely at Rose's and Dave's faces."

She looked.

"Do you see what I see?" I asked.

"What do you see?"

"I see makeup on Dave's face."

Jackie got closer. After a second or two, she said, "I think you're right."

"Now, let's see about Rusty."

Rusty came on and gave some scores and talked about Sooner preparation for the fall. He also gave equal time to Oklahoma State at Stillwater. There were always complaints that the Oklahoma City papers, radio and TV stations gave more time and space to the O.U. Sooners than to the O. State Cowboys. The complaints were probably right.

"He's wearing it too," I said.

"You're right," Jackie said.

I went to the phone and called Channel 10. I told a young female voice in the newsroom that I was the lieutenant governor of Oklahoma and that it was essential that I talk to Rusty as soon as he got off the air. He knows me, I said, and I gave my home telephone number. I said it was important state business.

The theme music was still playing when our phone rang a few minutes later. It was Rusty. He was delighted to hear from me, and what could he do for me? I told him I needed to ask him a few off-the-record questions. Shoot, Coach, he said. He called everybody Coach, just like Janice Alice called everybody Dove. It was his on-air trademark.

"Do you wear makeup on the air?" I asked.

"Sure. Is that a violation of an Oklahoma law, Coach?" He laughed.

"No. Next question." I did not laugh.

"Shoot, Coach."

"Do all TV reporters wear makeup? Men, I'm talking about."

"Yes, sir. They all do. They have to. Otherwise we'd all look like we had diarrhea or something. Gray, washed up and out."

"Now, this is important, Rusty."

"Shoot, Coach."

"Do male TV reporters carry compacts?"

"When they go out to do an interview or a story away from the studio, yes. Yes, indeed."

"Compacts like . . . well, like ladies carry?"

"You got it. I even have one myself that I use when I go out to Norman or wherever for a story."

"*You* carry a compact?"

"That's it, Coach."

"Thank you, Rusty. You've been very helpful."

"Do you mind telling me what this is all about? You thinking about passing a law saying TV guys can't carry compacts? . . ."

"I can't say any more. State security. Thank you."

We hung up. Jackie was watching me like I was a lunatic who might suddenly grab her neck and start squeezing.

"I have never heard a conversation like that before in my whole life," she said. "I think it's all getting to you, Mack. Maybe you should take some time off. Grown men should not go around talking about carrying compacts. Particularly grown men who are the lieutenant governor of Oklahoma."

I ignored her and turned out the light. I had to concentrate on what I knew and didn't know about the

Okies. And about Archibald Tyler, CBS News, Oklahoma City.

I awoke to a ringing. Oh well, I thought, for once the alarm had won. I was an early riser just by nature. But I always set the alarm for 6:15 just to make sure. And I almost always beat it awake.

It was the phone, not the alarm.

I turned on the bedside light. My digital clock said 5:48.

It was C.

"I am very sorry to tell you they just got your man, Boomer Webster," he said.

"Got him?" I wasn't fully awake. I didn't understand.

"Killed him. A bomb connected to the ignition on his bus. Blew him to bits."

Blew him to bits. That's what the hand grenade did to Pepper in Korea.

"Maybe it's not all a crock after all, Mack."

There's nothing to worry about. You are not in danger.

You sure?

I swear on my oath as lieutenant governor of Oklahoma.

Within minutes, an OBI man was there to take me, siren screaming and red lights flashing, to the Downtown Airpark on South Western just a block off Reno. C. was there. We climbed aboard a small OBI plane and took off for Ardmore.

7

On My Oath

It was the fifth plane ride I had taken since I became lieutenant governor—the seventh in my life. The first two were campaign trips when I flew out and back to Guymon in the Panhandle with Buffalo Joe. Since then there had been trips to Altus, Frederick, Bartlesville, Broken Bow, Vinita and back to make speeches or cut ribbons. I had cut a lot of ribbons. Mostly for football locker rooms, mobile libraries, hospital wings, K mart shopping centers and restaurants. The smallest ribbon-cutting I ever did before JackieMart–South Western was for a barbecue place in Adabel. One of the men at our church was opening his first business, a two-burner, one-window hot-pit carry-out. Brother Walt agreed to bless it and he said the least I could do was come down from Oklahoma City and cut the ribbon. So I did.

Most of the requests for my presence came through Buffalo Joe's office. He couldn't make something, so I was asked to fill in. I didn't mind. Most of the trips were made by car and I loved driving around.

And I got to where I didn't really mind the small

airplanes. The OBI's plane I was on was bigger than some. It was a seven-seat single-engine Cessna 207 Skywagon.

Brother Walt always said God's intention was not for human beings to fly. He said if that had been the case he would have given us the proper equipment to do so. Brother Walt did not believe metal machines with moving tails and wings and gasoline engines were the proper equipment. He was in his late sixties and had never been on an airplane. "That's the reason God's still got me breathing," he said. "He figures anybody smart enough to stay off airplanes deserves a good, long life."

Jackie and I had a theory that Brother Walt would always be alive because he was the Second Son of God. Jesus was first, but instead of sending him back as the Bible said, God decided to send the Second Son instead.

I very much wished he was with me in that Cessna 207 Skywagon on the way to Ardmore.

The sun was just up over the Arbuckle Mountains and Turner Falls as we flew into the Ardmore airport, which was south of town on Lake Murray Road. I hated even to think of what I was going to have to do, say and see.

A state policeman met us at the airport and took us, siren and red light going, to the scene. To that place on B Street, a side street around the corner from the bus depot where Boomer had met his death. It was a terrible scene.

The bomb had blown away the driver's seat and the steering wheel of Boomer's red and white bus. There was a hole in the roof above and in the floor below. Most of the steering wheel and all of the accelerator and the brake pedals were gone. So was the left side of the windshield. The rest of it was cracked and just hung there. Everything was black and bloody.

All kinds of official-looking people in suits and ties and police uniforms were walking in and around the bus. They took pictures. They put pieces of things in clear plastic bags. They talked in whispers like they were in church or at the library.

They had taken Boomer away. The FBI and the OBI and the county sheriff and the Ardmore police had agreed an autopsy had to be done. An autopsy on what? I tried not to imagine what Boomer must look like now. But I couldn't help it. Did it blow off both of his legs? What about his stomach and his chest? Was that red face destroyed? Where did those two pillow hands end up? Did they find everything? How do they know that? Have they reassembled him at the mortuary?

They were the same horrible questions I asked when they brought Pepper's body back to Adabel. It was in a coffin. Brother Walt identified him for the Marines so Jackie wouldn't have to. I never looked. I wanted to, but I couldn't.

I tried to imagine what it had been like for Boomer. He must have sat down in the seat of that bus maybe still a bit sleepy. What had he had for breakfast? Were his wife and kids up to say their last good-byes? Have a great day, Dad. Don't take any curves too fast, and for goodness' sakes, remember to stop at all railroad crossings. He must have been thinking of the long day that lay ahead of him. Of driving over to Durant and then back, and again, and again until it was dark and he had done it both ways five times. How many passengers will there be going east this morning? How many coming back? Would they have a lot of baggage? Would the bus break down? Would it be a good day for Boomer Sooner Coaches? How many of the passengers would be freebies, people who told him they didn't have the money for a ticket today?

Then he turned the ignition key. Pushed the tiny

starter button. Did he hear the explosion first? Or did he just feel something coming up at him from the floorboard? Did he smell anything? Did he have time to cry? To say, Well, that's my life for now. See you later.

See you later, Boomer. I am so very sorry.

C. and I said nothing to each other as we walked and looked. He left me for a while to go have conversations with some of the men in suits and ties. When he came back over to me, I was standing by the side of the bus staring at the hole in the ceiling above the driver's seat.

"Last night about nine-thirty, a guy came and wired it," C. said. "Our guy was down the street in a car and watched the whole thing. The FBI had a guy who sat in another car and watched. So, apparently, did everybody else in American and Oklahoma law enforcement. They all assumed he was a mechanic who had come to fix the bus. No big deal. Routine. The guy had on a mechanic's uniform and was carrying what looked like a tool kit. He rigged it with a device hooked to the starter and drove away."

C. waited for some reaction. I had none. What was I going to say? You mean, Director of the OBI, that your agents and everybody else's agents sat and watched while a bomb was placed on this bus? You mean your people are so stupid they did not even think to check out the mechanic? They are so stupid they did not think to check with Boomer to see if he had sent a mechanic to fix his bus?

"Who was the killer?" was what I said.

"Mafia. The real kind. Probably a specialist they flew in from Dallas or Kansas City or New Orleans."

"Why?"

"Because they bought the crock that Boomer here was the leader of their new competition. It's the way they handle competition."

"How could they have believed that about Boomer? He was just a simple guy with a little bus."

"Because they're stupid, Mack. They're psycho stupid."

There was a response that was right up there at my teeth ready to come right on out, but I stopped it. I did not say: Unlike all of us on the other side who are so psycho smart?

"Any chance of catching the bomber expert?"

"My guess is that he's long gone by now. We're doing what we can to trace him in and out. But I wouldn't bet a Whopper on getting anything."

There's nothing to worry about. You are not in danger.

You sure?

I swear on my oath as lieutenant governor of Oklahoma.

Boomer's house was one half of a small white frame duplex with a porch and blue shutters. The address was 202 A Street. It was five blocks south and west of the bus depot, three blocks due west from where the bus was parked, where Boomer had died. There was a pack of news people out in the street in front of the house. The police wouldn't let them go to the door. Several of the reporters yelled questions at C. and me as we walked through. "Later," said C. I said nothing. There was only one reporter I was interested in seeing. Archibald Tyler, CBS News, Oklahoma City. He wasn't there. At least I didn't see him.

Boomer's wife was named Betty. Betty Ann Webster. She was a big woman like Boomer was a big man. But the killing of her husband had made her seem small sitting there on a torn, dirty purple and green couch in the tiny front room of their house. There were two or three kids and several people crowded in there with her.

She had on a blue dress. Her hair was long, dirty blond, and it wasn't combed.

I told Mrs. Webster who I was and I took her right hand in mine.

"I am very sorry, ma'am," I said. "He was a good man."

Her eyes were light blue. She put them up and on me like two .22 rifle barrels.

"You remember his telephone call the other night?" she said. "You remember what you told him? You remember how you said there was nothing to worry about? You remember how you told him he was in no danger? Do you remember all of that?"

"Yes, ma'am. I will remember it for the rest of my life. I am so very sorry."

"That won't bring him back."

She had been crying. There was red around the edges of her eyes and there was a sopping wet handkerchief in her hands. But she wasn't crying now.

Her anger with me had stopped it.

"Is there anything I can do to help you now?" I said.

"Nope."

"Is your minister here?" I looked around the room for somebody who might be a preacher. Nobody looked the part.

"We don't have a minister," she said, as though that were my fault, too.

"What denomination are you?"

"Holy Road. But we hadn't gone since we came here." Her voice was suddenly apologetic. Like she was hoping that I wouldn't tell anybody that they hadn't been going to church. She was a good woman. It was obvious why a good man like Boomer had married her.

"Would you like to have a Holy Road funeral service for Boomer?"

"Yes, I guess. Yes."

"I'll take care of it."

"Get a good preacher," she said. "Boomer liked good preachers."

"I'll get you the very best, ma'am."

I excused myself and went to the telephone in the kitchen. It was a messy kitchen, full of plates and pans that weren't quite clean, trash that needed emptying, walls that needed painting.

Brother Walt came to the phone immediately. I told him the situation.

"I'll be on my way in ten minutes. Tell the bereaved widow I should be at her house in two hours and fifteen minutes," he said.

Brother Walt, the Second Son of God, to the rescue. Always.

"I can have an OBI plane sent for you," I said.

"Pass. Thank you."

I went back into the living room and told Mrs. Webster that the finest Holy Road minister in Oklahoma— if not the world—was on his way.

I shook her hand and motioned to C. to follow me back outside. We stopped on the porch. More than thirty reporters with cameras and microphones were out on the street now, being held back by police. The word had spread, obviously, that C. and I were inside.

"I think you should say something to the creeps," C. said from the front porch, "or they'll never leave us alone."

"You're the professional," I said. "You talk."

"The Chip put you in charge."

I looked out again for the puffy face of Archibald Tyler. I found it. He was there. In the very back.

"I see Tyler," I said to C.

"Me too. I figured he'd probably still be in his hotel room playing with his compact. The man's a psycho deviate.'' I had not told C. about my makeup revelation.

"Are your people still watching him?"

"With utmost skill and dedication. I'll find out in a few minutes what he's been up to this morning."

We walked out to the press people. They crushed around us with their microphones and cameras like I had seen them do so many times to so many important people on television. It was the first time I had been one of those important people.

"All we can say now is that it is a terrible tragedy. We have no concrete leads on who did it. When we make an arrest to take any action we will let you know."

I tried to walk away. But as at the press conference at the capitol, they wouldn't let me. They shouted their questions: What's the connection to the Okies? Was Boomer Webster an Okie? Is it true he was under police surveillance? Is the FBI here? What kind of explosive was used? Do you expect other killings?

"I can only say this," I shouted finally. "Boomer Webster definitely was not an Okie or anything else connected to any criminal activity. Period."

"Why was he killed then?" somebody screamed.

"I can say no more at this time," I said.

If C. and his agents had not been with me, I might have put my hands to my head and cried the second we got back into the car.

I never dreamed being lieutenant governor of Oklahoma would be anything like this.

It was hours later in a state policeman's room at the Best Western out on Interstate 35 that I finally had a few personal minutes with Brother Walt. I told him I needed to see him in private before he drove back to Adabel. He had gone to see Mrs. Webster, and arranged for a funeral at the First Church of the Holy

Road in Ardmore and got it all donated by the funeral home, the florist and everybody else, on the grounds that Boomer Webster was the innocent victim of organized crime. He had also successfully encouraged the manager of the bus depot and the florist to tell a reporter for *The Daily Ardmoreite* that they were starting a fund to help Boomer's widow and family. Send donations to the Webster Family Fund, c/o *The Daily Ardmoreite*, they said to the reporter. Fine, he said. It would go in the paper that way.

Typical Brother Walt. Typically Wonderful Brother Walt.

He was so important to us it was hard to imagine what life would be like without him. We had had only one brief glimpse of that possibility. He had given us only the one scare during a baptism. Or I should say, God gave us only one scare about Brother Walt. It was back when I was county commissioner.

Jackie, the kids and I were all sitting there on the third row in our regular pew. It was all set for baptism Sunday. There was an enclosed glass case–like thing behind the altar that was a lot like a huge aquarium, similar to the one I saw in the Holy Road equipment catalogue, only older. The deed was performed by filling it up with water and then immersing the heads of the confessed sinners, one at a time, and pronouncing them cleansed of sin and ready to walk the Holy Road to Glory. I thought the whole thing was stupid. To avoid having to do it myself, I told Brother Walt I had been properly dunked in Lufkin, Texas. It was the only real serious lie I ever told Brother Walt. I just did not see the connection between believing in God and Jesus and being nearly drowned. Still don't.

Brother Walt always did his dunking at the end of the Sunday-morning service. This morning there were five big high school boys lined up in single file for the treatment. Each had a white towel hood contraption over his shoulders to keep from getting completely soaked. Brother Walt first had each one of them publicly declare his hot desire and willingness to do it and reminded them of their duties as Christians and Holy Roads. Then came the action.

"In the name of the Father, the Son and the Holy Ghost," said Brother Walt, grabbing Boy One's nose with one hand, the back of his head with the other, "I hereby cleanse you of your sins and baptize you in accordance with the precepts and orders of the Church of the Holy Road."

He pushed the kid's face down into and under the water. There was a swussh noise. He held it there. Count of one. Count of two. Back up.

"Hallelujah!" yelled somebody out in the congregation, followed by a chorus of "Amen!" and "Praise God!" and such.

Boy One, water dripping off his head and nose, disappeared and Boy Two stepped forward. Brother Walt said and did the same thing to him. But when he pulled the kid back up, I saw a pained frown strike Brother Walt's face. Like he had just swallowed something awful.

But it seemed to pass and he grabbed for Boy Three.

And collapsed.

I was the first one up there. He was barely conscious and was breathing hard and sweating and clutching his chest. Dr. Cap Samuelson, who was sitting several rows behind us, was there a couple of beats later.

"Heart," he said almost immediately. He ordered me and those high school boys to pick Brother Walt up and get him to a car. "Can't wait for an ambulance."

Brother Walt was barely breathing when we got him to the county hospital four blocks away a few minutes later.

He was put on a bed with wheels and rolled away by a small army of nurses and doctors in white.

It was more than an hour later that Dr. Cap came out and told Brother Walt's wife, Martha, and the rest of us that Brother Walt was alive and that it looked like he would survive.

Within a week Brother Walt was almost back where he started. Or at least that was the way it seemed to me. He was still in the hospital and in his pajamas, but everything else about him was normal. Meaning he was still the Second Son of God.

"Do you have to think about being and acting so good or does it come naturally to you now?" I asked him one afternoon during visiting hours.

"It's no different for me than for you or anyone else, Mack," he said.

"You are the Second Son of God," I said.

"We are all the Second Son of God."

"Where is that said in the Bible?"

"Everywhere."

"I sometimes have evil thoughts."

"So do I."

"I do not believe you."

"God is Great."

Brother Walt was out of the hospital and back to work nearly full-time and full-speed within three months. There was no way to tell that he had ever been sick a day in his life, much less had a heart attack and almost died. I could not imagine a more healthy man anywhere on the Holy Road to Glory.

I decided it was all a stunt by God to throw us off track. I believed Brother Walt would live forever.

Still do.

"What's the Lord wrought here, Mack?" he asked me now at the Best Western in Ardmore. It was a hot day, ninety-seven or so degrees outside. We each had a cold can of Dr Pepper in our hands. He was sitting in a chair by a small round table near the air conditioner. I was standing across the room from him. I was too antsy to sit down.

I told him the whole story. Some of it he already knew from the papers and television, but I quickly filled in the rest. Then I got to the hard part.

"This man Boomer called me. He told me he was scared. I told him not to worry. I told him he was not in danger. Now he is dead."

"You didn't kill him. There is no blood on your hands. So there should be none on your mind. You made sure eyes were kept on him. How could you know they would be the eyes of idiots? Policemen are dangerous because they speak in the name of the law and think they're special. I have always said, Beware of anybody whose kind begins with the letter *p*, Mack."

He had never said it to me before. Politicians? Painters? Psychiatrists? Pilots? Pilgrims? Presidents? Pitchers? Preachers?

"I don't think there is such a thing as an Okies crime organization," I said. "Russell Frank says it's a figment. C. says it's a crock. So do I. I'm convinced of it."

"Who is the liar—the figment-maker, the crock-er?"

"That CBS reporter Archibald Tyler."

"Black hair like a spaniel? Smiles like a singer? Sounds like rust?"

"That's the one. He made up this whole Okies story. I know he did. I am certain now. There is no other explanation."

"What's the explanation for why he made it up?"

"Don't know."

"Well, God is Great, Mack. If you don't know that, then you don't know anything. People do bad things for reasons and only for reasons."

"I don't know how to proceed. . . ."

"Where is he?"

"Here in Ardmore now. He's covering the bombing. . . ."

"Go to him. Confront him. Tell him what you think. Maybe he'll fall on his knees and confess."

"That only happens in your business."

He looked at his wristwatch. "Got to run. Two young people need me to marry them at eight back in Adabel." He stood and came over and grabbed me by the shoulders. "Confront him, Mack. The Lord says he who shrinks is small."

"When did He say that?"

"You challenging the Greatest Holy Road Preacher in Southeast Oklahoma on scripture?"

"No siree. No. How could I ever do that?"

"God is Great."

And he left.

8

The Blue Arrow Meeting

C. convinced me it was smart to wear a "wire," a tiny tape recorder with a microphone the size of a shirt button. He said it would be smart in case something ever ended up at a courthouse with a bunch of mad-dog psycho lawyers fighting among themselves. But I brushed away C.'s suggestion that I also carry a .38-caliber pistol under my coat. Archibald Tyler was not going to attack me with his microphone, I told him. I was going to be in no danger.

The late Boomer Webster was supposedly in no danger either, C. replied.

I did let C. and his agents take me to where Tyler was. They said he was at the Ardmore bus station filming his report for that night's *CBS Evening News* with Roger Mudd Substituting for the Vacationing Walter Cronkite. An OBI agent had reported on the two-way radio that he saw Tyler take a woman's compact from his pocket and make up his face.

"I'll bet he's wearing pink panties and a slip under that blue suit of his," C. said, after we drove up across the street behind the depot. We parked in front of an old tin-and-machine shop. There was Tyler standing with a microphone in his hand on the rear loading dock. A crew of people with a camera and a sound-recording thing were capturing his every word for CBS and America.

"C., there is one piece of evidence that I must now reveal to you," I said. "My own investigative efforts have uncovered the fact that all TV men carry a compact and put on makeup."

"That does not surprise me," C. said.

"I mean, it's normal, not abnormal."

"I mean, that does not surprise me."

The cameraman and the others started to disassemble their equipment. I got out of the car and walked toward Tyler.

His made-up face crinkled up like he was in pain when he saw me. He started walking the other direction, around the building toward Washington Street. I upped my pace. I caught up with him at the northwest corner of the depot building.

"I need to talk to you," I said. "It's urgent."

"Not urgent enough, Mr. Lieutenant Governor," he squeaked. He took three more steps.

"You made this whole thing up," I said as steadily as I could. "And I can prove it."

He stopped. He turned. His face was now in a terrified smile. Like he had just been scared by a joke about ghosts.

"You are a murderer, Tyler," I said. "You killed Boomer Webster as sure as if you planted that bomb on his bus."

"Where can we talk about this?" His voice seemed suddenly even higher and squeakier than usual.

I pointed toward an Oklahoma Blue Arrow Motorcoaches bus parked on a lot next to the station. "We can sit in that bus,'' I said. It was a new model of the big GMC parlor coach The Thunderbird used to operate. Oklahoma Blue Arrow was Tommy Walt's company, of course. It went west from Ardmore to Waurika, and then to Lawton or Wichita Falls, and north to Oklahoma City on old Highway 77 and the interstate through Davis, Pauls Valley, Lexington, Purcell and Norman. It also had a run on northwest to Enid, Woodward and finally to Garden City, Kansas, where it connected with Continental Trailways for Denver and points west. The buses also ran east out of Oklahoma City to Tulsa and to Shawnee, Seminole, McAlester and Fort Smith, Arkansas. Both Continental and Greyhound had tried to buy Blue Arrow for years, but the good Oklahoma City owners always refused to sell. This GMC had the traditional paint job. Navy blue and white with two huge blue arrows joining points at dead center of the front of the bus, the arrow staffs running down each side with the feathers of the two arrows coming together at the dead-center rear.

I motioned for Tyler to sit down in the first seat on the left. I closed the bus door and sat down across the aisle from him, right behind the driver's seat. I wanted him on my right, where the good eye was.

Now I could see the makeup on his face clearly. It made him look like he was on a magazine cover.

''You invented the Okies,'' I said again. ''You made them up as surely as they used to make up fairy tales. I do not know why you did it and I do not know why you thought you might be able to get away with it, but I know you did it.''

He wouldn't look at me for more than a blink or two at a time. He was thinking. I kept talking.

''You have done harm to this state and to its people, of course. But you have caused the death of an innocent man. A decent man. A man who wanted only to drive that old bus of his back and forth between here and Durant. A family man. A man . . ."

"Boomer Webster was not part of this," he said. "I had thought maybe a Mafia type or two might get hit, but I never ever thought something like this would happen. I did not intend for any innocent people to get hurt. Coming down here and covering the death of this Boomer Sooner man was the most difficult thing I have ever had to do."

His words were running together. He was talking way faster than normal broadcast speed.

I'm sure he expected me to say something. I had nothing to say. Except, Good God Almighty!

He continued. "I also never planned for anyone, you or anyone else, to figure it out. Under my plan I would confess . . ."

"We're not the hicks down here you figured we were," I said. It was a stupid, childish thing to say. The man was talking incredible craziness and I was defending hicksism!

"No hicks talk, please. Remember—I'm from Coffeyville, Kansas."

"So was the Dalton Gang," I said, again without thinking.

He had me. "You must be from Kansas. Nobody but Kansans know about the Dalton Gang." He said it with real pleasure. Like he had just found a friend. People from Kansas are like that. They love running into somebody else from Kansas.

"Yes, I am. My grandmother lived in Coffeyville, in fact."

"You ever go to the Dalton Gang Museum on East Eighth?"

"My grandmother was best friends with the lady who took tickets there for years. I went there fifteen times. Maybe twenty."

"It's something to grow up in a place where the most famous people in its history were bank robbers."

"Well, I am from Medicine Bend, up in the central part of the state, and I'm about its most famous native."

"Been there many times. Your high school was named after Carrie Nation, right?"

"Right. 'We're the home of the Carrie Nation Hatchets and the lieutenant governor of Oklahoma,' is a common thing for the people to say to visitors."

"How did a boy from Medicine Bend, Kansas, grow up to be the lieutenant governor of Oklahoma?"

"It's a long story." The conversation was not going the right way. I was beginning to enjoy this awful man with the closing-screen-door voice. It was time to get it back on track. Back on business. I just wished he hadn't been from Kansas.

"What you have done is worse than anything the Dalton Gang did," I said before he had a chance to say he had time to hear my long story. "Maybe they'll build an Archibald Tyler CBS News Museum in your honor after you're gone."

"Gone?"

"To the penitentiary."

"You're probably right about the museum. Just being a good-local-boy-makes-good network correspondent has made me something important in Coffeyville. But as a villain I'll be an even bigger deal. People will drive out of their way to see the house where the Villain Network Correspondent spent his formative years. Maybe they'll put a plaque on the little white house where we lived. We lived right behind the high school near the old Union Electric interurban barn."

"Do you mind if I ask how you got away with getting this made-up story on the *CBS Evening News*?"

"It was easy. Routine."

"CBS doesn't care if their reporters are telling the truth?"

He stood up. He was smiling, relaxed and happy.

I stood too. I was frowning, nervous and confused.

"Reporters are the finders of the truth. I come back to the office and I say, 'Sources say there is a new crime group.' They say, 'Great job, Arch.' "

"You don't have to sit down with Roger Mudd and explain why you say there's a new crime group?"

"No, sir. That would be an insult to me and my profession."

"What about with Walter Cronkite when he's there?"

"No, sir."

"Not with anybody who says, 'Arch, who says there is a new crime group?' "

"If I say my sources said it, they say, 'Great, Arch.' "

"How can a news organization as big and famous and national as CBS run its business like that?"

"That's how they all do."

"*All* of them?"

"Got it."

"This is unbelievable. Is this how they're doing the Watergate story, too?"

He ignored that and stepped down into the bus stairwell. "I think you're wrong about me going to a penitentiary. Lying on television is not against the law."

"Well, I may just ask the governor to call our legislature into special session so we can make it illegal, at least in the Sooner State of Oklahoma."

"Isn't he all tied up taking care of that dome problem right now?"

He grabbed the lever to open the door. "Look. Mostly what I'm going to be doing is going to the bank to deposit great sums of money."

"I don't follow that." I said it because I didn't follow that.

"You will shortly. I promise."

"What about Boomer?"

"I told you that was an unfortunate accident. I did not expect the Mafia to move that fast and stupidly. I never identified Boomer Webster as being an Okie. Everybody just added up two and two and came up with five—an innocent man, an innocent victim. I am very sorry about that."

"I am very sorry about that too."

"I understand there's a fund being set up for his family. I will make as big a contribution as I can. I promise," Tyler said.

He opened the door.

"All that remains to be decided is the timing, Mr. Lieutenant Governor," he said. "I await your angry whistle-blowing. There are plenty of reporters still in Ardmore. Hold a news conference at the Best Western. Whatever is your pleasure. Got it?"

Got it. This man was deadly, deadly serious. For a few split seconds I thought maybe—just maybe—he was pulling my leg. That he might suddenly say, Okay, hick Lieutenant Governor, it's all a joke. There really is an Okies and I am an honest man.

"You are the worst man I have ever known," I said. I wished I had taken up C.'s offer to bring a .38 with me.

"Correct. I am a terrible person. I will soon become American broadcast journalism's first publicly confessed villain. This has been an important meeting here on this Blue Bird bus. . . ."

"Arrow. Blue Arrow. Oklahoma Blue Arrow Motorcoaches. My son works and pitches for them. . . ."

"Yes, Blue Arrow. You must remember everything that has been said here between us on this Oklahoma

Blue Arrow Motorcoaches bus. Did you secretly tape it? You should have. You will become a celebrity. My fellow reporters are going to want to know the whole story of how you uncovered national television's first liar.''

He stepped down to the ground. I followed him. I wanted to tackle him, to hold him until a lynch party arrived, until the cavalry came over the hill.

"Have you made up a lot of stories like this?" I asked.

"This is my first big one." He said it very calmly, like whatever storm there was had now passed. Now he was just explaining himself to the ignorant, boring, one-eyed lieutenant governor of Oklahoma.

"You've made up a lot of little ones?"

"Just quotes and minor things."

"Quotes?"

"Sure. I come to the conclusion the attorney general may buckle to pressure from Billy Bob Senator from Nebraska and not prosecute a terrible person in Nebraska for tax evasion. I report, 'Justice Department observers say Billy Bob Senator's friend may escape prosecution for political reasons.' "

"You're just quoting yourself?"

"Got it."

"And you don't tell anybody at CBS News."

"Got it."

"And nobody at CBS News asks you, 'What observer?' "

"Got it."

There we stood, outside the door of that Oklahoma Blue Arrow GMC parlor car. Talking like two normal people. Like there was nothing special going on. It reminded me of a seminar I had gone to in the summer up in Ponca City about how to rid running stream water of solid sewage and then reuse the water for drinking water.

"Have you always made up things?"

"The first time I think was when I needed a quote for a weather story. I was on *The Topeka Capital-Journal* rewrite desk and I had to do a story about the temperature hitting a hundred degrees for the first time that summer. They wanted color and people in the story, so I made up people who said they had tried to fry an egg on the pavement in front of their house and who talked about sticking their heads in plastic bags of ice. That kind of thing. No harm done."

"They were all lies."

"Got it. I even made up the names and then checked the Topeka phone book to make sure there were no real people by those names around."

"This is awful. Do *all* reporters lie?"

He grinned. His voice deepened as deep as it would go as he said, "Oh, no. Only me. I am an aberration. A rotten apple in an otherwise perfect barrel."

"I am going to the phone now and turn you in to Roger Mudd."

"Be my guest, sir." He reached in his right pants pocket and pulled out a coin. He flipped it over to me. I caught it by reflex. It was a nickel.

"Get out of the sight of my one good eye," I said. The seminar on solid waste was finally over.

"Yes, sir." He started to walk away and then turned back. "You control the schedule now. Under my plan I would have let it play out another week or so. I wanted to let the talk of journalism awards for my outstanding reporting get started first. *Time* and *Newsweek* are both planning profiles for their press sections. The *Times* has even interviewed me. But things could change. If I don't hear anything from you I will just go ahead and make my confession when the time seems right. It wasn't my original plan, but now I think I really do prefer its coming from you. But that is your decision. If you want to call Mudd. Fine. Call Cronkite on his boat. Call the ghost of Edward R. Murrow. Call Nixon. Call Jesus and the pope. Call anybody you like. As you know, I can be reached temporarily at the Park Plaza in Oklahoma City or through CBS News, Washington.''

He turned his back on me and walked away.

"You are a disgrace to Kansas and to Coffeyville!" I yelled after him.

I am not a violent man. I really am not. But I swear, if I had had a .38 pistol right then, I would have drawn its sight up to my one good eye and drilled him square in the back of his head.

I was sure Brother Walt could find me a line of scripture to justify it fully to God in heaven and to Man on earth.

An OBI agent back at the car said an emergency message had come through for me from Oklahoma City. It said I was to call Glisan at the Union Bus Station as soon as possible.

I went to a pay phone on the corner.

"Trash has gone too far this time, sir," Hugh B. Glisan said in an almost calm voice. "I know he is your son and I know he is a pitcher, but he cannot work in my bus depot for one more minute. But before I kicked him out on his butt for now and for good and forever, I felt I ought to inform you first. That is what I am doing now."

"What did he do, Glisan?" I asked. And held my breath for the answer.

"He spray-painted cusswords on the walls in the men's crapper."

"How bad were the words, Glisan?"

"As bad as they get, sir."

"I didn't know he knew those."

"Trash is a pitcher."

"He must have picked them up working in your bus station."

"Sir, please!"

"What color was the paint?"

"Blue."

"Greyhound or Blue Arrow?"

"Kind of in between. Lighter than Blue Arrow blue, darker than Greyhound."

"Where is he now?"

"He's locked himself in one of the crapper stalls."

"Go tell him I am on the phone and want to talk to him."

"Yes, sir."

I listened to silence for a couple of minutes. I wondered what gene my friend Tom Bell Pepper Bowen had put into his son that caused him to act this way. I wondered if Pepper was watching and listening to all of this and laughing his fool head off. Hey, Mack, tell him to go steal a Flxible Clipper or something, take a bath and he'll feel fine in the morning. That's how Pepper talked.

"Hi." Tommy Walt sounded perfectly normal.

"Why did you spray bad words on the restroom walls, son?" I asked.

"Lefty called me and said I was starting on Wednesday. It flipped me out. I figured I would never have to start again."

"That's a normal reaction."

"Normal? It's normal to grab a can of blue spray paint and spell out . . . well, you know . . . all kinds of words after you've been told you're going to start?"

"Pitchers have been doing crazy things like that since the game of baseball began. Are you willing to clean up your mess?"

"Yes."

"Let me talk to Glisan."

Glisan got back on. He agreed to blame it on the fact that Tommy Walt was a pitcher and give him one last chance.

"I got to tell you the truth, though, sir," he said. "And I do it with Trash standing right here listening. You are not doing him any favors pulling him out of these things time after time."

"Thanks for the truth, Glisan."

"You're welcome, sir."

While I was there at the phone I called Jackie at Jackie Mart–South Western. Collect.

"T. Ray Powell is an idiot," she said of her young store manager without even answering my hello. "He prances around here like he's running a Safeway in downtown Tulsa, yelling at the workers and the customers and the gods and the devils and the weather and the sky, and it's driving me crazy."

"Fire him."

" 'Fire him.' Is that all you have to say?"

"Got it."

"Where did you pick that up? 'Got it.' You sound like somebody else."

"I am somebody else."

"Who?"

"Your son just spray-painted cusswords on the walls of the men's bathroom at the Union Bus Station."

I heard her gasp. "Did he hurt himself?"

"You don't hurt yourself spraying cusswords on walls, my dear."

"It's that baseball again, isn't it? He did it because of baseball. I know he did. Baseball's an evil spirit in his soul, Mack."

"Speaking of evil spirits," I said. And I told her

about the conversation I just had with Archibald Tyler, CBS News, Ardmore, Oklahoma.

"What's he really up to?" Jackie asked. "Why is he suddenly so anxious and ready for you to tell the world he's a liar?"

"I haven't figured that out yet," I said.

"Did you ask him point blank? Did you say, 'Mr. Tyler, What exactly are you up to?' "

"No, I didn't. I was so stunned by what he was telling me it just slipped right by. . . ."

"Buffalo Joe called here an hour or so ago looking for you. Said to remind you of the Dome Commission meeting at nine in the morning. Said the world's number-one expert on domes was coming from Cincinnati. Then he told me about a man from Waurika with an idea for putting a searchlight on top of the dome that would be so powerful it could be seen on a clear night from every city, town and farm in Oklahoma. Said it would be a unifying inspiration to all Oklahomans.

"How long does this craziness about the dome go on, Mack, before people start laughing in every city, town and farm in Oklahoma?"

Like I say, it was not easy being the Second Man of Oklahoma, father of a crazy bus baggage agent/stuff pitcher and husband of the smart-mouthed originator of drive-thru grocery stores all at the same time.

9

First Things First

C. was in my office at the capitol the first thing the next morning. He came with the transcript of a telephone conversation. Tyler had made the call from his Park Plaza room the second he returned from Ardmore the night before. It was to a New York City number and lasted less than half a minute.

MAN'S VOICE: Hello.

TYLER: Marty? Arch Tyler here. Sorry to bother you at home so late.

M: No problem. What's up?

T: Get the copies of the synopsis ready to go. It could break tomorrow.

M: Tomorrow? Great. Call me. I'll hand-deliver them. The personal touch. I'll get the bidding started immediately.

T: Good. Thanks.

M: Don't spill too many details. The details are the product. Don't give away the product.

T: Got it.

M: I've got the armored cars and yacht salesmen standing by.

T: Sure. Bye.

"Our people have identified the guy as Martin Alpert," C. said. "He lives on a street called Central Park West, New York City. He is a vice-president of the William Morris Agency."

"Related to the cigarette people?"

"No relation to Philip as far as we know. We've been told William Morris are agents who represent movie stars, celebrities and other types," C. said. "It's all beginning to add up, isn't it?"

"Add up to what?"

"That's precisely what you and I have now got to figure out, Mack."

"Well, it's first things first, Mr. Director," I said. And I stood up to go. "I have got to run around the corner to a most important meeting of the Dome Commission. You are free to sit there in that chair to figure it out without me."

"I like this capitol building flat on top the way it is."

"Precisely," I said.

It was officially known as the Governor's Commission to Complete Construction of the 1914–15 Plan for the State Capitol. There were six members. The governor, the lieutenant governor, two members of the Oklahoma legislature—one from the Senate and another from the House—and two private citizens. Arneson and Heket were the two private citizens. Buffalo Joe wanted no surprises. He chose two legislators with the hope that they would be unable or unwilling to come to the commission meetings. The senator was from Boise City in the Panhandle and he seldom came to Oklahoma City except when the legislature was in session, which was only for ninety days beginning in January. The House man was from Vinita and he suffered from emphysema, so he stayed mostly under an oxygen tent in Vinita, which was up in the northeast corner of the state near the Missouri border.

But everybody came to this meeting, only the second we had had, because Dr. Malcolm T. Swift was coming and some decisions were going to be made. Wayne Al Meyer, the young architect, had found Dr. Swift. He was a professor of civil engineering history at the University of Cincinnati and was the number-one expert on domes. He knew more about domes than anybody in the world, having studied most major existing domes throughout the world and having been a consultant to the construction of most new domes built since the early 1950s. When it came to domes he was the man. Meyer concluded and Buffalo Joe's staff agreed, in fact, that he was the *only* man. He had no peer. No equal.

Dr. Malcolm T. Swift was not what I expected. He was not tall, bald and boring. He did not wear those queer little metal-rimmed glasses. He did not speak with a Massachusetts or foreign accent. He was a short, pudgy, smooth-skinned, gray-haired and absolutely delightful man of fifty-five or sixty. He could have passed for a junior high principal or an uncle anywhere. Even in Oklahoma or Kansas.

After brief introductions all around, we took seats at a long conference table. A slide projector was at one end of the table, a huge white screen at the other. It was the same room where Joe normally conducted his news conferences and other meetings that were too big to fit in his office. The capitol maintenance crew had arranged the several soft leather chairs around the conference table in the center of the room.

Joe got things under way with a statement of purpose, a reminder of why we were all here. "Oklahoma is known the world over as the unfinished state," he said. "We are known that way because our state capitol building is unfinished. The time has come to finish it. The time has come to crown Oklahoma. Crown Oklahoma, gentlemen."

"Where are we known as the unfinished state?" said the senator from Boise City. "I have been all through New Mexico, Colorado and Kansas, my wife's people are from Nebraska, my daughter is away at school in Missouri, and I have two aunts in North Carolina and a third in Jackson, Mississippi, and I have never ever in my life heard of anybody referring to Oklahoma as the unfinished state. All I ever hear people say about us has to do with songs about surreys with a fringe on top and the Sooner football team."

"It's news to me too," said the House member from Vinita. He took a deep breath from a tube connected to a portable can of oxygen he had by his chair.

"I have heard it called that from one end of this nation to the other," said Arneson.

"Seldom a day goes by that I do not hear someone say, 'We are the unfinished state of Oklahoma,' " said Heket.

Joe glanced around at me. It was my turn. "Same here," I said. "Same here."

Thus we took our first vote. It was 4 to 2 that Oklahoma was known as the unfinished state.

Then Joe introduced Dr. Swift, who stood up and started talking like he had known us all his life.

"Dome, dome, who needs a dome? I hear that question asked today just like our forefathers heard it asked when they designed the nation's capitol in Washington. Just like the Romans and the Greeks and the Phoenicians and the Texans and the Kansans and the Kentuckians and the Cutler County Iowans heard it asked before they put domes on their senates, palaces, statehouses and courthouses. Dome, dome, who needs a dome?''

He signaled an assistant to turn out the lights and turn on the slide projector. Dome after dome after dome came up on the screen. Purple domes, silver domes, metal domes, glass domes, concrete domes, fancy domes, tacky domes, cheap domes, expensive domes. Domes on shopping centers and churches, on city halls and museums, on office buildings and university administration buildings.

''Imagine, if you will,'' said Dr. Swift, ''a world without domes.''

The same pictures came up again. Only this time the dome on the top of each building had been eliminated through the magic of an artist's airbrush. All were domeless. We saw the U.S. Capitol and the others the way they would look without a dome. It was striking and sad.

''Now, gentlemen, look at this,'' said the dome expert of the world.

There, several feet above our heads, was a shot of our capitol building without a dome just as it was in real life at that moment. Then another of it with a silver dome. A golden dome. A dome of tinted blue glass. A dome of bright white light. A dome of hundreds of small green lights.

Then he slowed it down.

''Here's how your capitol could look from the south at midnight.'' Slide change. ''From the west at dawn.'' Slide change. ''From the north at high noon.'' Slide change. ''From the east at dusk.''

Each picture was with a different but impressive kind of dome on top.

''Oklahoma has a choice to make,'' said Dr. Malcolm T. Swift. ''It can join the rest of the dome world or continue to show a flat and naked sight from all points of the compass.

"Are there questions at this juncture?"

The senator looked at the representative, who coughed. They had clearly been had, and knew it. Neither wanted to be a party to keeping Oklahoma a flat and naked sight from all points of the compass.

"All right, how much will it cost?" asked the senator.

"Depends on what kind you want and what function you wish it to perform," said Dr. Swift.

"We just want it to look nice. No functioning," said the representative.

"Well now, well now," said Buffalo Joe, who was at that moment as happy as any man I had ever seen in my life. "A wide variety of potential functions have been suggested for our dome that would crown Oklahoma. The suggestions have come from people all over this state, big and small alike. Schoolchildren in the Panhandle, elderly citizens in the awful cities, young people of all colors and creeds, of all colors and creeds."

He was looking right at Dr. Swift now.

"Tell us, Dr. Swift, what would be the possibilities of this dome being a self-supporting project?"

"You mean, could it pay for itself?"

"Yes, sir."

"It's possible, if there was some money-making function it could perform in addition to its being a dome. There have been revolving dome restaurants at World's Fairs that remained in business long after the fair was over. A book or gift shop of some kind might be feasible. Possibly even an exclusive specialty store along the lines of a Neiman-Marcus. The problem is strictly one of transportation and logistics."

"What?" coughed the state representative from Vinita.

"Transportation and logistics," Dr. Swift said. "Getting the people up to the dome and accommodating them and their needs while they are there and then returning them to the ground."

"How about making it a nondenominational chapel?" said the senator from Boise City. "It would certainly put the worshipper nearer his God to thee."

"We have had a suggestion that a huge beacon of light be put up there," said Joe. "A light so bright it could be seen on a clear night throughout the state."

"I'm not sure there is a light that bright," Dr. Swift said, "but we can look into it."

"The astronomy department at O.U. is pushing to have a big telescope up there," Arneson said.

"It would have to be shared with O. State for it to sell, right, Senator?" Heket said.

"Ummmhuh," said the senator.

"Are you saying it's possible we could put this dome on without it costing the taxpayers of Oklahoma a cent?" asked the state representative.

"That's it, that's it," Joe said. "Like a toll road. We sell Crown Oklahoma revenue bonds to build it and then retire the debt with the revenues through the years."

All six of us members of the Governor's Commission to Complete Construction of the 1914–15 Plan for the State Capitol looked around and down and across the table at each other in a kind of silent exchange of "Well?"

Joe looked squarely at me. I knew what he wanted and I did it.

"I move then that we ask Dr. Swift here to take the suggestions we have given him and to come back to us as soon as possible with a specific plan of action along the lines we have just discussed," I said. "Crown Oklahoma."

"Second the motion," Arneson said. "Crown Oklahoma."

"Are there any questions?" Joe said. "Hearing none, members of the commission will now vote on the motion of the lieutenant governor. We will now vote on the motion of the lieutenant governor. All in favor, please raise your right hand."

Six hands were raised.

"Well done, gentlemen. The motion carries unanimously. Dr. Swift, the future of our dome is now in your hands.

"Crown Oklahoma, Dr. Swift."

When I returned to my office, C. was still sitting in the same chair in front of my desk.

"I figured it out," he said. "He's got more to gain from being a famous liar than from not being."

"He never planned to get away with it?"

"Precisely. He would make up a story, admit he did it and become rich and famous because of it. That New York agent-type is in charge of the rich-and-famous part," he said.

"You're right. That's got to be it," I said. "He's probably going to write a book. That's the synopsis he was talking about. *How I Made Up a Big Story About Oklahoma and Got Rich*, by Archibald Tyler, CBS News, Washington. That must be the product they were talking about."

"Precisely?"

"Precisely. I think."

"Have you got somebody at the OBI who talks like they're from the North?"

"Paisley, in public affairs. He's from Pawhuska but he can impersonate anybody. Does magic tricks for Lions and Kiwanis and schools. Kids love him. He can make a sound like a monkey and a tiger and a lion so realistic you'd think you were at a zoo.''

In less than five minutes Paisley was with us. Five minutes after that, Paisley was at my desk waiting for the phone to ring in Tyler's hotel room. It was rigged to a speaker phone, so we could hear both ends of the conversation.

"Mr. Tyler," said Paisley in an accent that sounded pure Up There to me. "This is Jackson Newton with Random House." A woman in the reference department of the Oklahoma City public library had given me the names of three big book-publishing companies. Random House was one of them. I chose it because she said it was run by Bennett Cerf, the guy on the *What's My Line* television show. C. came up with the name Jackson Newton. Had the right-type sound, he said.

"Yes, sir," Tyler said to Paisley/Newton. There was warmth and excitement in his squeak.

"We hear you have a bombshell of a book in the works, is that right?''

"You hear right. Marty Alpert of William Morris is representing me on this and everything else.''

"Everything else?''

"Lecture bookings. Movie rights. The whole thing.''

"Well, we will certainly get in touch with him. Question, though, please, if you don't mind.''

"Sure. I'm delighted you're interested.''

"We hear it has to do with the truthfulness of your Okies crime gang story. Is that right?''

"Possibly.''

"Well, in all due respect, that doesn't quite add up to a bombshell book on the face of it, if you understand what I mean." Paisley was doing well.

"It will become clear as a bell in a day or so, I can assure you of that," Tyler said, taking all the bait.

"Watch and read your favorite news outlets for details. Be particularly on the lookout for news from Oklahoma."

"You mean there is something special to come out about the truthfulness of your story?"

"Yes, sir. Very special. Unprecedented, you could even say. It's a first of a kind."

"Sounds exciting. We'll be in touch with your agent."

"Good. Thanks."

I looked over at C. Theory confirmed. And then some.

"Now what?" he said to me after thanking and dismissing Paisley.

"Precisely," I replied.

At that moment I heard the deep rich trooper tones of my father. He was in the outer office saying hello and how are you to Janice Alice Montgomery.

Then he was at my office door.

"I could not stay away," he said. "Not with my Lieutenant Governor Son in such a state of misery and forlornness."

Forlornness?

Dad was a tall, husky man who kept all fat off his body by running two miles and doing fifty push-ups and thirty sit-ups every day of every year. Most of his dark hair was now gone, but he still had enough to comb. He was a handsome, dedicated man. Kansas was lucky to have him as one of its highway patrol officers. Why he did not remarry after my mother died I did not know. I had never asked him.

I introduced C. and Dad to each other.

"You're a legend in Kansas and all of law enforcement," Dad said to C. as they shook hands. "I'm delighted you are with my boy on this Okies business."

"It's what I do, Lieutenant," C. replied. "We will be delighted to have your help."

"It's all unofficial, as I am sure you understand."

"Precisely. Just a father giving a helping hand to a son."

"Precisely," I said.

10

Make It True

We were in Brother Walt's office at the First Church of the Holy Road in Adabel. All of us. C., Dad, Sheriff Russell Jack Franklin, Brother Walt and I. It was in that office that Brother Walt and I told Jackie that Pepper was in jail and at Brother Walt's suggestion had decided to join the Marines and go to Korea rather than stay in jails here and elsewhere on fourteen arrest warrants from three states. And it was here the Marine captain officially informed Jackie that her husband, Tom Bell Bowen, Private, USMC, had been blown to bits by a hand grenade.

Now, more than twenty years later, I was here because I didn't know what to do about stopping Archibald Tyler, CBS News, from becoming rich and famous by making up a terrible story about Oklahoma on national television.

C. was sitting on the couch with the sheriff. They were comparing notes about some thug from Indiana who had been picked up in Antlers in a hot Mustang with a trunk full of dope stuffed into red, white and green balloons with "Merry Christmas!" stenciled on them. The state policeman who stopped him got suspicious because it was July.

I was talking to Dad about reporters making up things. He told me about the time he picked up the paper and saw himself quoted saying, "It looked like World War Three in there." It was in a story about a Korean War vet from Lindsborg who drove down to McPherson and shot up the feed store where his ex-girlfriend worked. Nobody was hurt and Dad had gotten there long after the kid had been subdued by local officers and the thing was over. He hadn't said, "It looked like World War Three in there," or anything else to any reporter. Dad ran into the guy who wrote the story several days later and he said he needed a quote and figured Dad wouldn't mind.

Dad and I had spent Saturday with C. Mostly we drove around playing the tapes of my Blue Arrow meeting with Tyler and of Tyler's phone conversation with the man from William Morris. We were in C.'s OBI command car Lincoln. We drove from Burger King to McDonald's and around. It was mostly in silence after the first three hours or so because we ran out of ideas, of things to talk about.

We discussed bringing Buffalo Joe into it. Shouldn't I go right now to the governor's mansion and tell him about this? Why not let him make the decision? Let him figure out a good way to blow the whistle on Tyler? No, said C. The Chip wants to stay as far away from this as possible. Besides, he would think of something stupid.

And besides that, I said, we already have enough really smart guys like us on the case who are thinking of all kinds of smart things to do.

Like calling Roger Mudd. It was decided to do it. We pulled up to a Conoco station and I placed the call to him at CBS in New York, where I had called him before. I charged it on my state telephone credit card. Why did you call Roger Mudd in New York City on a Saturday afternoon from a pay phone at a Conoco station? I could hear the state auditor asking. To save the State of Oklahoma, I could hear myself replying. But Roger Mudd was off on Saturday and the woman who answered would not give me his unlisted home telephone number. She wouldn't even tell me if he lived in New York City or somewhere else.

So we drove off and thought and talked some more. No matter what we said, it always came back to the iron-hot certainty Tyler was going to get away with it. There was nothing I or anybody else could say in a whistleblowing announcement that would take away from the fact that he was going to get rich. Just like he planned it.

Finally, around five in the afternoon I decided to call Brother Walt. I called from a Derby Oil station.

I told him in three or four sentences what an awful fix I was in. "Be here after church tomorrow. The Lord will help us think of something," he said. "God is Great."

"Does the Lord ever help people think of executions?" I asked, just to make his Saturday night interesting.

"He invented executions, Mr. One-Eyed Mack," he said. Which made *my* Saturday night interesting.

We flew down in the OBI's Cessna 207 Skywagon in time for church. I made C. go to the service with Dad and me. He said it was the first time, except for lawmen's funerals and weddings, that he had stepped inside one in over thirty years. Walt sermonized against false idols and false witnesses and said one sometimes posed as the other so be careful. The huge sanctuary had been freshly repainted all in white enamel, and it looked and smelled fresh and beautiful. Brother Walt had married us there in front of a crowd of four people, all of them from Brown's Hotel Coffee Shop, where Jackie worked. He had also sent what was left of Pepper to his grave from here after a service attended by a handful of Marine recruiters from Tulsa, some American Legion men and a few others. Nobody in Adabel had had a chance to get to know him before he went off to die for America in Korea, a place none of us had ever heard of before.

I shook some hands of some old friends and then guided C. and Dad up to Brother Walt's office on the second floor. We walked by the two huge portraits that struck Pepper and me that first day we came into the First Church of the Holy Road, Adabel, Oklahoma. One was of Jesus Christ, the other of Brother Walt. They were of equal life-size.

Brother Walt had said he would join us as soon as the church was completely clear. Like the ship captain, he believed the preacher should always be the last to leave his sanctuary after a worship service. It was his suggestion that I invite Russell Jack to join us. C. agreed. He's crooked but he's smart, C. said. That's why we hadn't caught him yet.

I didn't take long to lay out the situation for Brother Walt, when he finally joined us. I had brought the tapes to play for him. We listened to them twice all the way through.

"Why didn't you ask him why he was doing it, Mack?" Brother Walt said when the tapes finished the second time.

I said, "He's doing it to get rich."

"No, sir. No, sir. Everybody thinks everybody does evil things for money. They do not. They say it's for money because they don't want to admit why they're really doing it."

"I am not following you, Brother Walt. I am not following you. He wants to be a famous villain so he can write books and make speeches and movies and go to the bank. You heard what he said."

"Something's missing. He's mad about something. He's really mad about something. Something has turned him so mad it made him crazy. But he doesn't want to admit that, so he says it's for money."

"How can you say that?" C. asked.

Look out, C.

"I can say that, sir," said Brother Walt, "because I know it. And when I know something I say it. As the Great Broadcast Journalist Liar himself said over and over to Mack on the tape, got it?"

"All right, all right," C. said. Smart people do not fight with preachers in their own church in front of other people. C. was a smart people.

"God is Great," said Brother Walt.

Either Brother Walt and C. were oil and water that would never mix or they were going to go together like the two strong, sticky things you mix together to make epoxy glue.

"All right, let's talk solutions," said Brother Walt. "Last night on the phone you seemed to be suggesting executing this TV man. Is that what you really want to do, Mack?"

The other three men in the room sat upright.

"I said that to get your attention," I said. "What's that you said about the Lord inventing executions?"

"That was to get *your* attention. Although punishing the wicked with death is not an uncommon occurrence in the Bible. Eye for an eye, ear for an ear and so on."

I reached up to my empty left eye socket. It was a reflex. I glanced at C. His hand was up where his right ear used to be.

C. spoke. "What if the Mafia killed him just like they did Boomer Webster?"

"Could you arrange that?" Brother Walt said calmly.

"As easy as arranging for two sausage biscuits with cheddar cheese to go at Burger King."

"God is Great. Now how would you explain that to yourself? You are a man of the law. How would you explain taking that law into your own hands? Wouldn't that be for you the worst sin that can be committed in the State of Oklahoma and the United States of America?"

"Calm down. I was just trying to get your attention."

"I am half a mind to impose a citizen's arrest upon you myself and turn you over to the sheriff here for prosecution on charges of plotting to take another man's life."

C. looked over at me and at Dad and the sheriff for help. He got none. People were always on their own with Brother Walt. I had grown to like C. very much. I suddenly felt sorry for him. Tangling with Jesus' brother on his own ground was about as treacherous as it gets.

"I merely wanted to make sure every possible course of action was on the table," he said finally. "Spare me psycho preachers."

"Spare me all people whose kind start with *p*," said Brother Walt.

Brother Walt then took me through the exact words I might use in my announcement exposing Tyler and his lies. I did it a second and a third and a fourth time, with Dad and the others offering suggestions on how to phrase things to make Tyler seem as bad as possible. The problem was that the worse Tyler was pictured, the better off he would be. It played right into his hands.

That awful fact stayed with us as it had with C., Dad

and me during our drive through Oklahoma City on Saturday. And not even Brother Walt could make it go away.

"It just does not seem right that a man should be able to get away with something as atrociously evil as this," I said for the thousandth time since Friday. "To make up a lie and then turn around and get rich on that lie. . . ."

"God is Great," said Brother Walt. "I have it!"

He walked behind his desk and sat down. He put his hands together, closed his eyes tightly and said, "Gentlemen, let us pray."

We all closed our eyes and bowed our heads. Even C.

"Our Heavenly Father, thank you again. Thank you again for being our savior. For showing us the way to Glory. For delivering us to a method to combat this evil. Amen. God is Great."

Brother Walt stood. His face was alive.

"Gentlemen," he said in his best pulpit baritone, "there is a way to thwart this man. The Lord has just told me what it is."

He walked around from behind his desk. We all stood and moved toward him like he was a light and we were bugs.

"If there is no lie, he has nothing to confess, correct?"

"Yes. But there is a lie. Many of them. His whole Okies story is a lie from start to finish," I said.

"Make it true. Make it true and you make him through."

Make it true and you make him through.

"Did you say, 'Make it true and you make him through'?"

"God is Great."

Dad, C., Russell Jack and I moved back to our re-spective seats and sat down.

Make it true and you make him through.

It took a few more minutes and a few more words for it to sink in fully.

It then took another two hours to come up with a plan. It was the most exciting and enjoyable two hours I had spent since watching that first Okies report on the *CBS Evening News* with Roger Mudd Substituting for the Vacationing Walter Cronkite.

I knew we had made the right decision when I saw *Time* and *Newsweek* Monday morning. Both had stories in their press sections about Archibald Tyler, CBS News. Both said Tyler had scooped not only the jour-nalistic world but the worlds of law enforcement and the State of Oklahoma as well. *Time* had sickening quotes from him about how "a story like this comes along only once in a reporter's lifetime and thank God it finally happened for me."

Newsweek got me to thinking about Brother Walt's "why" question. The story said Tyler had always hoped he would be picked from the correspondent ranks to begin climbing "the golden ladder" to anchorman, but it hadn't happened yet because his voice was too high. It said he sounded like a fingernail being scraped across a pane of glass and people couldn't bear to listen to him for more than a minute and a half or two minutes at a time. "The Okies scoop might help him overcome this unfortunate voice-register handicap," said *Newsweek*.

I read it out loud to C. and suggested maybe, just maybe, it was Tyler's anger over his voice discrimina-tion that triggered all of this.

"All of this because some psycho reporter squeaks when he talks?" C. mumbled. "Forget it."

We were once again in the backseat of his Lincoln.

This time on the way to Boomer Webster's funeral in Ardmore. It was raining and C. said it would be safer to drive for two hours than fly for thirty minutes in the Cessna 207 Skywagon. We had gone by the Jackie-Mart–South Western on the way out of town and picked up coffee, cinnamon rolls, the magazines and the morning papers.

Crazy T. Ray Powell was on duty. "Drive that car slower to this window or drive it not at all," he snarled at OBI agent Smith when we drove up to pick up our orders. I felt like lowering the back window, pointing one of C.'s submachine guns at him and saying, "Pardon me, but my wife, Jackie, asked me to come by this morning and fire you."

The Daily Oklahoman and the *Tulsa World* were full of the Okies story, of course. They had been since Tyler first splattered it on our state from the *CBS Evening News*. But what caught my eye that morning were two columns from up north. One was by a guy in Washington, D.C., named Buchwald and the other was by a New York man named Baker. They both wrote funny-type columns about the events of the day. What they both chose to write about this day was the Okies.

Buchwald wrote an awful thing about how the governor of New Jersey called in his top aides and ordered them to start a New Jersey crime organization like Oklahoma's. Why didn't one of you think of something like this yourself, he demanded. Look at the publicity they're getting. Beaten out by Oklahoma, for pity's sakes! I want a New Jersey mob on the ground by first thing in the morning! That's an order!

Baker's was an atrocious story about a native Oklahoman who, because of the Okies stories, had become an outcast at his place of employment, a small machine shop in Wausau, Wisconsin. In despair and shame, he finally burns his Sooner T-shirt, throws away his University of Oklahoma Marching Band recording of "Boomer Sooner," removes his autographed photo of Coach Bud Wilkinson from the top of his dresser drawers and shreds his Will Rogers joke book.

"They actually pay people to write psycho trash like that?" C. said. "All those people up there are psycho."

He waved in a more or less northeasterly direction.

Toward Arkansas and Missouri. And beyond.

There were thirty-five or forty of us there with Mrs. Webster and her children in the sanctuary of the Ardmore First Church of the Holy Road. I recognized the mayor of Ardmore and a county commissioner or two. Some of the others were bus drivers. I saw at least one in the uniform of Continental Trailways, two Greyhounds and four Oklahoma Blue Arrows. C. said the rest were probably psycho reporters.

Archibald Tyler was not there. At least the man had some sense of decency. Some.

A middle-aged woman, accompanied by a middle-aged man on the organ, sang "Rock of Ages." That was appropriate because Boomer struck me as being a rock of a man. There were six or seven large floral wreaths donated by the florist's shop that made the place smell like a perfume counter. Inappropriate. Boomer was not a man of perfume.

Brother Walt ran the whole show. He brought us to our feet to sing all four verses of "Bringing in the Sheaves," which he said was Boomer's favorite hymn. Then he sat us down while he read some scripture about what a great place heaven was. Streets lined in gold, houses of jewels, smells of frankincense.

Then he read a brief biography of the deceased.

"William Allen Webster. Born of Christian parents in Osage County on August 23, 1940. Grew up a man of the red soil of northern Oklahoma. Grew up a man who knew the value of work. A man who played by the rules. A man who dreamed of owning his own business, of being his own boss. A man who lived to see that dream come true. A man who will be remembered always as a friendly driver behind the wheel of his own beautiful motorcoach. As a man who never turned away somebody who needed to go where he was going. William Allen Webster passed to his reward on July 12. He is survived by his devoted wife, the former Betty Ruth Reddin of Bartlesville, and three loving children, William Junior, Margaret Lou and Martha Lee, all of the home.''

Passed to his reward? The man was blown to bits by some Mafia hood. He was blown to bits because a television reporter made up a story. What kind of reward is that?

We sang three verses of Boomer's second most favorite hymn, "Onward, Christian Soldiers," and then it was sermon time. I knew what Brother Walt was going to say. He always said pretty much the same thing at funerals. It's all God's will. It's all for the better. Life is fantastic in heaven. More fantastic than the one down here, in fact. So dry your tears and let's hear it for the afterlife. He said it with conviction and he said it well. But it was a crock.

Boomer Webster's death was the third big one in my life. The first two to die were my mother, who died of a burst appendix when I was twelve, and Pepper. Each death was unbearable awfulness. All deaths of healthy, well people are. Period. Forget there being some spirit afterward that floats off to a better life in heaven. Death was a lousy thing for everybody—the dead person most particularly.

Brother Walt always said I would feel differently if I was the one who was dead.

I told him that was a crazy way for a preacher to talk.

God is Great, he replied.

That's what he always replied.

"We mere mortals must know in our hearts that God has a plan for us. And that plan includes going off to heaven, to his Home, to a Glory. . . ."

That's all I heard of his sermon that morning in Ardmore. I just tuned him out like he was a radio, and concentrated my mind on Dad and this evening's edition of the *NBC Nightly News* with John Chancellor.

Dad was taking Step One in our plan to Make It True.

T. Ray Powell had finally had some kind of richly deserved breakdown at JackieMart–South Western, so Jackie was tied up for the evening. I went by the bus station to check on Tommy Walt.

"Trash is already gone," Glisan said. I suddenly wanted him very much to quit calling my son Trash. "He cleaned up the mess in the crapper. You want to see it?"

"No, thanks," I said. "What do I owe you?"

"The moon. You owe me the moon, sir."

"I don't have the moon on me. How about taking a ten-spot?"

"Forget it. I kind of like Trash myself. He's a good kid. I just wish he wasn't so crazy."

"He's a pitcher. He can't help it."

"I know."

I went back to my office and called home to see if Tommy Walt wanted to join me somewhere later for dinner. No, thanks, he said.

"You don't like being called Trash anymore, do you, son?" I asked.

"How would you like being called Trash, Dad?"

"They used to call me The One-Eyed Mack, so I know the problem."

"No, you don't. 'Trash' and 'The One-Eyed Mack' are in different leagues, Dad. Different ballparks. Different sports. Different worlds."

I had asked C. to join me back in my office at the capitol to watch the *NBC Nightly News* with John Chancellor. But he said why not go to the Sears in Shepherd Mall and watch it. Sears? I replied. He said he got a big kick out of going in there and seeing something important on all twenty-two of its TV sets at one time. How do we know they'll have all twenty-two on NBC? I asked. They know me there and if I want all twenty-two on NBC, they'll do it, he replied.

"Is twenty-two an exact number?" I asked C. on the escalator down to the basement floor of the TV and appliances section. His two young agents had gone down ahead of us to make sure that no Mafia hit men or other psychos were lying in wait for us.

"I counted them myself," he said.

Sure enough. There were twenty-two, and they knew him there. A man who looked like he was in charge welcomed C. and me to his department. C. said something about NBC, and the man and two clerks quickly raced among the TV sets until all twenty-two were on Channel 5, our NBC affiliate in Oklahoma City.

C. and I stood there with two or three customers and watched a couple of commercials on twenty-two TV sets. Then came John Chancellor and the *NBC Nightly News*. First came a Nixon denial. I didn't pay much attention to what he was denying. The second story was ours. Dad had scored.

"There is a development in the Okies mob story," said Chancellor, another of my favorites I had been sorry to miss because of all my CBS watching. "Correspondent Rob Herson has the story from Oklahoma City.''

Herson was a young man in checkered sport coat and bow tie. His voice was deep, the opposite of Tyler's. On most of the TV sets his coat looked gray and black. On others, green and blue. On others, blue and purple. He was standing in front of our state capitol building next to the *Cowboy on a Wild Pony* statue. He was breathing hard like the end of the world was upon us.

"A disaffected member of the infamous Okies mob came forward today and talked exclusively to NBC News. Demanding that his name not be revealed, he agreed to make a statement about the activities of the crime organization that apparently came into being unbeknownst to all law enforcement agencies charged with the responsibility of combatting organized crime."

And there came up a picture of my father, the finest lieutenant in the Kansas State Highway Patrol. But you couldn't see his face. Only the back of his head in shadow. But the voice was loud and clear.

"I operate mostly in Arkansas, New Mexico, Missouri and Illinois. My specialties are truck thefts and dope. I steal the trucks, others put dope on them and others drive them to California and New York. All of us are from Oklahoma. But none of us live there anymore. Boomer's our leader. He's in hiding. But he said he would kill anyone of us who talked. I'm talking because I don't like what's happening to my home state. Somebody killed the wrong Boomer. But that's scary. Also, it's not fair

to blame the whole state of Oklahoma for just what
the few of us have done.''

Herson came back on the screen.

"We were able to talk to the man for only a few
minutes. Our efforts to ascertain his full background
and other information were not successful. He de-
clined to answer all questions. . . .
"Rob Herson, NBC News, Oklahoma City.''

C. had taken some money out of what he called his
Investigative Contingency Fund to pay for Dad's rented
Chevy from Avis and his room at the Holiday Inn on
U.S. 77 North. C. said he could also buy him some
extra clothes if necessary, but Dad said he thought he'd
brought enough of the right kind from Kansas. The
right kind were those that would make him look like
a psycho thug. I've had business with enough of them
in my life to know exactly what they dress like, Dad
said.

Sheriff Russell Jack Franklin was holed up in a Best
Western on the east side of town near Tinker Air Force
Base. His prey was a *New York Times* reporter. We
wouldn't know how he did until the morning.

We had a three-day plan. Three days to take Archibald Tyler's lie and Make It True.

C. and I left Sears with a skip and a jump. Step One,
Day One, done.

Smitty drove us around to JackieMart–Westend. I
handed a note to the young man at the window. It was
a note Dad would pick up later. It said simply, "Well
done, Lieutenant Dad."

We had worked out a complicated communications
system. Dad was to go to the JackieMart–Westend
every evening anytime after nine. He would ask the

clerk for a Milky Pay bar. The clerk would say, "You mean, Milky *Way*?" Dad would say, "Change it to a Butterfinger." Then the kid would hand him the envelope from me.

Milky Way was my favorite candy bar. Butterfinger was C.'s.

11

Last of the Ninth

My dear Jackie had a part to play the first thing the next morning. Right at nine o'clock I was in her office at the back of JackieMart–Westend. We closed the door and she placed a call to Roger Mudd at CBS News in New York, where it was Eastern Daylight Time and an hour later. I brought the phone number along from when I called him the week before.

She had the same trouble getting through I did. But once she said she was ''Boomer's girl'' a few times to a few people, Roger Mudd finally came on the line. I listened in on an extension.

''Mister Mudd, I only have thirty seconds to talk. Boomer's like a wounded bear. He's threatening to kill everybody. Me included . . .''

''What's your name?'' Mudd said. I knew it was Mudd because I recognized his voice. ''Where are you calling from?''

''. . . I'm ready to tell the whole story. I know 'em all. They're awful people. They're . . . Oh, my God, here he comes!''

And just like we worked it out, she hit the receiver cradle like she had been cut off.

I went over and took her in my arms.

"If running drive-thru grocery stores doesn't work out for you, ma'am, you can always get work as the gun moll for a crime boss," I said.

"Thank you, sir, but I have already been spoken for by the lieutenant governor of Oklahoma. He has the power to get me to do strange things, like call up Roger Mudd and tell him lies."

"He's a lucky man, that lieutenant governor."

"Speaking of luck, there's a man coming up to see me from Chickasha this afternoon," she said. "He wants to open up a JackieMart down there."

"JackieMarts are going to sweep Oklahoma and the world. People everywhere are just waiting for the chance to drive thru. You just watch."

"Maybe you're right, Mack. Wouldn't that be something?"

C. had already called and left a message by the time I got back to my office. "Bull's-eye," was the message. I called him immediately.

"Mudd had him on the phone in his room at the Park Plaza in a continental minute. He said to Tyler: 'This woman just called me. Said she was Boomer's girl. Said she knew them all. Said Boomer was like a wounded bear. We got disconnected. He must have just walked into the room.' The whole bit, Mack. Like a charm."

"What did Tyler say?"

" 'Is that so, Roger? Is that so?' And tough Roger said, 'You bet it's so.' "

"What about the NBC story?"

"Mudd didn't mention it. But Tyler's assignment man did. An hour earlier. He asked Tyler if he could find a similar guy and get a similar interview. He was nice about it, but it was clear he was ticked off that NBC had the interview instead of CBS."

"What did Tyler say to that?"

"Hardly a word. He just mumbled something about doing what he could. It's beautiful, Mack. Absolutely psycho beautiful."

"We're not there yet, C."

"The assignment guy also mentioned something about a *New York Times* story. So Russell Jack must have scored, too. Tyler said he hadn't seen it because it didn't arrive in Oklahoma City until late morning. He said it like maybe Oklahoma City was so far away in the sticks it's on another planet."

An hour later Janice Alice came in with *The New York Times*. She had gone out to the airport to get it. Our story was on page A14.

LOCAL LAW ENFORCEMENT OFFICIAL SAYS OKIES GONE TO TEXAS

An Oklahoma sheriff said yesterday that the so-called Okies mob has now moved south to Texas.

The veteran lawman said in an interview that the Oklahoma mobsters were working primarily out of Longview in East Texas and Abilene in West Texas. He said the ones he knew about were mostly truck thieves who drove large shipments of drugs, stolen cigarettes and other contraband to the two coasts.

"They are not as violent as people like you would think or like some of the stories have said," said the official.

The sheriff asked that his name not be used. "The Okies are a mean lot and I kind of would like to go on living," he said.

Law enforcement officers in Longview and Abilene, Texas, were contacted last night. All said they knew nothing of any crime organizations operating out of their cities. They also said there had been no sudden influx of Oklahomans as far as they knew.

"But it's hard to recognize an Oklahoman in a crowd," said one Texas police chief. "Most of them don't look that different than Texans."

The Oklahoma sheriff said local law enforcement officials in his state had had the Okies under surveillance for the last few years. There had been no arrests, he said, because there had yet to be any evidence they committed crimes on what he called "Sooner soil."

I ran out to the parking lot, jumped in my Buick and drove at top speed to the Jackie Mart–Eastside. I handed a note to the young woman at the window. It was for Russell Jack and it was only one word: "Hallelujah!"

He would come by later and ask for a pint of chocolate chip ice cream. The woman would say, "Sorry, we have chocolate swirl but no chocolate chip." "Make it butter brickle then," he would say, and she would give him my note.

Chocolate chip was my favorite flavor of ice cream. C.'s was butter brickle.

An hour later one of C.'s young OBI agents went up to the fourteenth floor of the Park Plaza Hotel. He stuck a white envelope under the door of Room 1417. The room of Archibald Tyler, CBS News, Oklahoma City.

Inside that envelope was a crumpled Xerox copy of a carefully typed "Electronic Surveillance Report" from the Oklahoma Bureau of Investigation. C. had typed it up himself. Xeroxed it himself. Crumpled it himself. Put it in the envelope himself.

It was dated the day after the Tyler report that iden-

tified the new Mob as being from Oklahoma. The tap
occurred at 11:10 A.M.

The report said:

MAN #1: Who squealed?

MAN #2: Well, it ain't me. Maybe you?

#1: No way. I like living too much.

#2: What about Tailback Butch?

#1: Butch wouldn't know how to talk to no reporter.

#2: That leaves Jerry Linebacker and Whiskey Cor-
nerback.

#1: They're in Texas.

#2: You going to talk to Boomer?

#1: Kid me some more, will you? There's going to
be cops coming out of the faucets and the toilet
bowls by nightfall.

#2: Where is he?

#1: Same place he always is.

#2: I'll be in Longview by nightfall. . . .

#1: I'm going to see Momma in Chickasha and then
I'm going to Abilene till it blows over. Spread
the word for everybody to get under the hay and
stay there.

#2: Already done it.

#1: Bye then.

#2: Bye is right.

It had been a collaborative writing effort. C. and I
wrote it together coming back from Adabel Sunday
night. I was particularly proud of the expression "get
under the hay and stay there," which I just made up
sitting there in the car as we rode along.

C. and his troops stayed hard on monitoring Tyler's
telephone. His first reports to me were encouraging.
There was the news that Tyler put in calls to five

sheriffs around the state to see if one of them happened
to know who might have talked to the *Times*. None of
them did. The best of the lot was a conversation he had
with a guy out in the Panhandle who kept saying he
wished the crime out here was organized. "All our
crooks out here are too stupid to organize," he told
Tyler. "I'll bet they don't even know each other."
Asked if any of his local hoods had suddenly run off to
Texas, he replied, "Our crooks couldn't find their way
to Texas and we're only forty-two miles from the border."

Then came the call he made forty-five minutes after
the white envelope went under the door of room 1417.
It was to OBI director C. Harry Hayes himself.

"You been tapping the phones of the Okies?" said
Tyler.

"No comment," said C. "We never discuss ongoing
investigations. This is not Washington."

"Isn't that against the law without a court order?"
said Tyler.

"No comment," said C. "We never discuss our investigative methods and sources. This is not . . ."

"I've got a Xerox of an OBI Electronic Surveillance
Report. It's a report on what two guys said to each other
about this Okie business. They're Okies themselves."

There was silence.

"Well?" said Tyler.

"Well, what?" said C.

"What do you say to that?"

"No comment."

C. repeated every word and breath for me. He even
did a good imitation of Tyler's squeaky-door voice. I
laughed and so did he.

Then he said: "But it did not end well, Mack, I'm
sorry to say. There was one of those long pauses people
make sometimes while they think before they talk, and

he said, 'Mr. Director, have you ever had a case of somebody stealing some of your blank Electronic Surveillance Report forms?' I said no as forcefully as I could, and he said, 'They're not numbered, so how would you know?' I said to Mister Psycho Reporter: 'Look here, people do not come into the office of the Oklahoma Bureau of Investigation and steal anything.' And he dropped it and that was it.''

I paused, like people do sometimes while they think before they talk.

"Sounds like he smells a tiny rat," I said.

"Yep," C. said. "If not a tiny rat, at least a tiny kitten among the baby chickadees.''

"Did you go ahead with the Boomer note?''

"Yep. Smitty gave it to a bellboy over at the hotel thirty minutes ago.''

This was a message I wrote in large letters in blue crayon on an old piece of lined tablet paper. "Am about ready to talk. Will contact later. The Real Boomer.''

"Maybe that'll keep him on track," I said.

"My smeller tells me it's going to come down to you and God's friend Brother Walt. The two of you are going to make it or break it, to tell you the truth.''

"My smeller's telling me something like that, too.''

"You going to do your big number tonight?''

"Tommy Walt is pitching. Got to see to that first.''

I didn't say it to C., but it was unlikely watching Tommy Walt pitch would take the whole evening. Sad to say.

"Want to go to the game with me?'' I asked.

"No, thanks. Promised the wife we'd hit the Burger King tonight. It's been ten days since I took her out on the town like that.''

Jackie went with me. When we got there, Tommy Walt was warming up along the left-field line just beyond the dugout. Jumper Allen, the regular catcher, was catching him. Jumper was a chatter man. Right here, Trash Boy! You got it, baby! Hey, hey, they'll never touch you! Hey, hey. He gave Tommy Walt the signal for curve. Tommy Walt threw a curve. And another. And another. Burn it in! Fastball signal. It popped into Jumper's mitt. Pop! I loved that Pop!

Jackie had gone on to our seats while I went over to behind the dugout so I could get a close look at Tommy Walt. He saw me. He gave the bill of his cap a slight pull. I could not tell whether he was happy to see me or not.

The Blue Arrow Buses were playing the OTASCO Jacks. They were in visiting gray uniforms trimmed in purple. The Buses, of course, were again in their home navy blue and white.

The home-plate umpire yelled, "Play ball!" and the Buses took the field. All except Tommy Walt raced to their positions. He walked slowly. Pitchers were supposed to walk slowly to the mound.

I joined Jackie in the Governor's Box behind the screen back of home plate. That was where I sat when Jackie was with me. It was called the Governor's Box because a governor had rededicated the stadium in the name of Wiley Post. Buffalo Joe had never come to a game as far as I knew. But it was free for me anytime I wanted to use it. But usually I just sat with Glisan in the Blue Arrows box.

As soon as I was seated, the PA announcer said as he always said, "We are pleased to have the lieutenant governor of our state with us tonight. Let's have a hand for him please, ladies and gentlemen." I stood and waved all around. And the people gave me a hand. It was one of the many pleasures and privileges of holding my office.

The lead-off batter for the Jacks was a tiny little guy

who played second base. My old position. Tommy Walt's old position.

The first pitch was high and outside. So was the second and so was the third. All were slow curves. The count was 3 and 0. Three balls and no strikes. Tommy Walt reared back and threw a fastball. It wasn't very fast and it was low and outside. Ball four. The tiny little guy who played second base ran to first on a walk.

The second hitter was the Jacks' center fielder. Good bunter. But he hit the first pitch on a line drive between first and second for a clean base hit.

Batter number three was a crowder. He stood right up almost on the plate. Tommy Walt grazed him with a slider.

The bases were loaded. No outs. Their star was up. Batting cleanup. Hands Allison. Best catcher, they said, in the history of Oklahoma semipro. Sick mother in Muskogee or he would have probably gone pro. The Phillies wanted him. So did the Giants.

I prayed. Please, Lord of the White Hard Ball, give my son his stuff tonight. Let him throw knucklers over the outside corners, snap-off curves over the inside corners. Let his change-ups dance and deceive. He is a good boy. Okay, maybe he does not have that much natural ability, but he's a fighter. He's out there pitching his heart out. He can't help it if you gave him short fingers.

The count went to 3 and 1 on Hands, and Tommy Walt, not wanting to walk a run across, threw a slider right down the middle.

Crack!

The ball headed for the left-field fence like it was a Springfield rifle shot. It hit the top of the fence and bounced back. Three runs scored. Hands Allison stood on second base with a double.

I clapped for the Buses and my son. He was kicking the mound with his cleats and fiddling with his cap and spitting chewing tobacco on the grass.

"Hang tough, Trash!" Hugh B. Glisan yelled from his seat two boxes away. "Give it to 'em, Trash!" Jackie was staring at Glisan. Trash. How would you like to be called Trash, Dad?

In a few seconds—it seemed like half the night— Lefty Anderson, the Buses' manager, came out of the dugout and began his slow walk to the mound. Lefty had played for the Tulsa Oilers, a Reds farm club in the old Texas League, and bummed around as a scout and minor-league manager for many years before he went to work for the Oklahoma Blue Arrow Motor-coaches.

He took the ball from Tommy Walt. Our son Trash walked off the mound and into the dugout and disappeared.

Jackie and I were in the car and a good five blocks away from Wiley Post Stadium before we spoke of Tommy Walt and what had just happened. I knew what was coming.

"Baseball is killing him, Mack," Jackie said. "You must get him to stop doing this to himself. He must get on with his life."

"He is on with it," I said. "He's doing fine at the depot now."

"You call throwing suitcases at passengers and painting dirty words on bathroom walls doing fine?"

"He's just a little high-strung. That's all. Goes with playing baseball."

"Craziness goes with playing baseball. He's got to stop it."

"He loves the game."

"How could anyone love what just happened to him? That awful fat little man Lefty, coming out there in front of everyone like he's king, taking the baseball from Tommy, taking him out of the game that way.''

''That's the way it's always done, you know that. In the big leagues they do it that way. To the biggest star pitchers of all, they do it.''

''Well, that does not make it right. And it sure doesn't make it right that Tommy Walt goes through it night after night like this.''

''He just didn't have his stuff tonight.''

''He never has his stuff tonight. How many times has he lasted more than two full turns? . . .''

''Innings.''

''Innings. He always leaves, and you always say, 'Well, he didn't have his stuff.' Any normal person can see he is never going to have his stuff, whatever stuff is.''

''It's what the pitcher puts on the ball.''

''Go buy him some better stuff then. Go to an OTASCO or a Western Auto or a Sears and buy him some. You're the lieutenant governor, they might even give it to you free if you asked them nice. They might even call your name and introduce you to the other customers on a PA system at the store. 'OTASCO is pleased to have the lieutenant governor of our state shopping in the store today. Let's give him a big hand now over there in the Baseball Stuff Department, where he's picking up some for his son who doesn't ever have any.' ''

My face was warm. She had gone too far. Way, way too far.

But she wasn't through. ''Trash,'' she said. ''Trash. 'Hang in there, Trash,' is what that fool yelled to Tommy Walt. 'Hang in there, Trash.' No son of mine is going to be called Trash anymore. And that's final.''

We had just arrived at JackieMart–South Western. She wanted to stop by for just a minute to check to see if T. Ray Powell was acting any better. She had given him another chance to pull himself together. To see if he really was intended for a career in the drive-thru business.

There were eight or nine cars in line when we drove up. Good. It's been like this all evening, T. Ray said. Good. Running short on Wonder whole-wheat. Can you make it through till closing? Yes, ma'am. Good. We'll restock first thing in the morning. Good. He seemed fine. Good. Everything was good at the JackieMart–South Western.

I picked up a copy of *Newsweek* off the magazine racks. She had just two weeks before added five magazines to what she sold drive-thru. *Time, Newsweek, U.S. News and World Report, Sports Illustrated, Sport, Popular Mechanics* and several women's magazines like *McCall's*. Some customers wanted her to stock *Playboy*, but she refused. No smut would ever be sold at a JackieMart, she said.

I walked back to Jackie's office and sat down in the comfortable overstuffed chair in the corner. I figured I would be here awhile. Her just-a-minutes were never just a minute.

But I had barely opened the magazine when T. Ray came rushing in. He had a look of horror on his plump twenty-six-year-old face. The kid really was not intended for this kind of work. You could tell by the way his eyes went from huge to slit. Nobody in the drive-thru grocery business should have eyes that went like that. It was a business that required steadiness. Even in the eyes.

"Mr. Lieutenant Governor, I am so sorry," he said like he had just run over my dog or child. "You got a phone call a while ago. The man said it was important. He said to tell you the second you came in, if you came in. I said I would. But I didn't. I completely forgot until now. It just slipped my mind.''

I put down the magazine and stood up. "It's okay, T. Ray. I haven't been here more than a minute or two. What's the message?''

"The message was: 'We lost. Call. C. We Lost. Call. C.' ''

Jackie got up from her desk so I could slide in and use the phone. In a few seconds I had C. on the line.

"Just a few minutes ago, Tyler made a reservation on the seven thirty-five Braniff in the morning for Washington. Then he called his head boss in Washington. He told him he was coming back in the morning. He said he needed to see him as soon as possible after he arrived. It was urgent. What about the story? the guy asked. There is no story, Tyler said. That's what I want to see you about. The guy on the other end was silent, like he was thinking, and then said, Okay, but it had better be important. It's the most important conversation you and I will ever have, Tyler said. And that was it.''

"What happened? I thought we had it won. Last of the ninth, nobody on, ahead by three.''

"Me too. My boys say he spent most of the evening in the hotel bar by himself, drinking martinis and eating cashews.''

"You think the cashews turned him around?''

"Hey, Mack. We lost it. The psycho's going to blow the whistle on himself and get rich, just like he said he was.''

"No, C. Let's not give up yet. We'll just do tonight what we were going to do in the morning.''

"Brother Walt and the bus too?''

"Yes. Why not?''

"Sure. Why not? I can have him up here on the Cessna in an hour and a half."

"Good."

Good.

12

Pick-up Window Two

It took a while to talk Brother Walt into flying in that Cessna 207 Skywagon. C. couldn't do it, so I had to call him too.

"It's not natural or biblical," he said to me. "There is no place in the Bible that says man was meant to fly in small planes in the middle of the night across the State of Oklahoma."

"The Bible says evil people should not be allowed to keep the evil fruits of their evil labors. It's a thirty-minute flight. Please. Just this one time."

"That's like telling a man to stick his head in the blast furnace just this one time."

Finally he gave in. But not until he had said, "Please tell the people of my church and the people of my town of Adabel and the people of my family that I did not do this voluntarily. Please assure them that I believe suicide to be a sin and that I did this under duress. Tell them that for all practical purposes you held a gun to my head, or I would not have willingly got on an airplane and flown to my death. Please tell them that, Mack. Can you do that for me and the Lord?''

"Yes, I can do that for you and the Lord."

"God is Great. Pray for me."

I did not pray for his safety. There was just no way God was going to allow Brother Walt to go down in flames in a Cessna 207 Skywagon. Brother Walt may not have had the faith and sense to know that. But I did.

It was already almost 9:30.

With the door to the mart closed, so T. Ray and nobody else would overhear, Jackie picked up the phone on her desk and called the Park Plaza. She asked for Room 1417.

"Tyler?" She said it perfectly. Like she was the toughest woman in the Sooner State of Oklahoma. "I'm the one who talked to Mudd. . . . Boomer wants to talk to you. He'll be out front of your hotel in an Oklahoma Blue Arrow bus at eleven-thirty tonight. You be there too. . . . You be there or somebody'll be up to your room in a continental minute to get you. Got it?"

She hung up.

"You were magnificent," I said. "Psycho magnificent." I meant it.

"He said he wasn't coming," she said. "He said he didn't know who I was or what was going on, but this was nuts."

"What's your guess? Will he be there?"

"I haven't even a guess." She picked up a letter from her desk. "Now there's a guy in Atoka who wants to open a JackieMart. I'm going to have to do something about this pretty soon, Mack."

"Franchise them, why don't you? Statewide, then nationwide, then worldwide, then spacewide."

"That's what I'm thinking too."

I dropped her off at the house and then drove on to the Park Plaza.

It was now time for me to do what I had to do.

I knocked on the door of Room 1417.

And I knocked again.

The door opened a crack. I saw Tyler's face and he saw mine.

"What do you want?" he said, in a tone that was much, much less respectful than it should have been of the lieutenant governor of Oklahoma.

"I have come to apologize."

"For what?" He opened the door almost halfway. He was dressed. Gray slacks and a blue dress shirt open at the collar. He had not gotten ready for bed. He was still at least thinking about 11:30. There was hope.

"For accusing you of making up the Okies story. That was a terrible thing to do and I just wanted you to know it. You are obviously a responsible journalist and I had no right to say what I did."

"Come in," he said. It was a large room. In addition to a king-sized bed, there was a little sitting area over by the windows. Two chairs and a small coffee table were there.

I saw his suitcase. It was on the stand at the foot of the bed. Packed. The suitcase was packed.

He motioned for me to sit in one of the chairs. He sat in the other.

"Mr. Lieutenant Governor, listen to me and listen to me hard. I told you once and now I'm telling you again. I made up the Okies. I invented them. I did it just like I told you before. Nothing has changed. They do not exist. I do not know where NBC and the others are getting their stories, unless they're making them

up too, but I am telling you there are no Okies. I
dreamed them up. Do you understand what I am telling you? I do not know what brought you here tonight,
but whatever, don't try to tell me there really are
Okies, because I know better. I am going back to
Washington in the morning to blow my cover and get
on with my plan. I gave you a chance to be a hero,
but you decided not to. That is your choice.''

He was talking fast again. Too fast. At first I thought
it was the martinis the agents said he drank earlier.
But it was his nerves. He was ready to come jumping
right out of his skin.

I waited for him to run down.

"Do you believe in coincidence, Mr. Tyler? Real
coincidence . . .''

"Forget it, Mr. Lieutenant Governor. Forget it. I
know what I made up. And what I made up was a
crime group named the Okies. You told me yourself
they were a . . . a something.''

"Crock. I said they were a crock. But I was wrong.''

"Now that really is a crock.''

"No, it is not. I jumped to some wrong conclusions.
We now have full proof that just such a crime organization as you described was born and lived in our
state. How our law enforcement people were unable
to penetrate them, I do not know. But thanks to your
reporting, the information got out. It turned the heat
under our folks and now we know about them. We
know all about them. Several have agreed to turn
state's evidence. We are taking full statements. They
are all saying the organization has mostly moved to
Texas, but there are still some Oklahoma remnants we
plan to eliminate. We may have some major investigative hearings by the legislature on statewide TV before it's over. We'll hear the whole story right from

the mouths of the Okies themselves. It would be wonderful if you would agree to testify."

He picked up a glass Park Plaza ashtray from the
table in front of us. He looked at it for a count of two
and then tossed it against the far wall. The ashtray
splintered into bits. "No!" he yelled. "No, no, no.
Shut up! I made them up! Listen to me! Listen!"

"I am listening to what a group of thugs are telling
our people. They are telling them that there is a crime
organization called the Okies."

"No way. Boomer? I made up that name out of thin
air. That poor man down in Ardmore is now dead because I made him up."

"There is a real Boomer. A real leader of this group
that calls himself Boomer."

"No! No way!"

I now threw all my dice.

"We finally found him. The OBI has a tap on his
phone."

That got his attention. "What's he up to tonight?"
he asked, trying hard to be casual about it.

"He's coming over here in an hour or so to talk to
you," I said. "At least that's what his girlfriend said
on the phone just now. He's coming on a bus. An
Oklahoma Blue Arrow bus."

Tyler stood up and went to the window. What there
was to see out that window were the lights across the
river south. On a clear day, I would guess you could
see almost all the way to Pauls Valley, fifty-five miles
away. There was little to block the view in central
Oklahoma. We've got some gorgeous real mountains
over in the eastern part of the state around Wilburton,
Clayton and Poteau and further west near Turner Falls
north of Ardmore. But the rest of Oklahoma is mostly
and wonderfully flat and raw. A lot like Kansas and
much of Texas. Only, our dirt is red except for some

parts in the southeastern part of the state around Adabel, where it's as black as anything you'll see in
Texas or Kansas.

"There's been one of those most remarkable coin-
cidences of history here, Mr. Tyler," I said, in as
comforting a tone as I could manage. "Maybe it was
mystical or psychic even, I don't know. You say you
did stories about an organization that you thought did
not exist. Okay, fine. I am truly prepared to believe
you when you say that. Truly, I am. You did it for
your own personal reasons, which I thoroughly de-
plore and condemn. But it turned out it really did exist. Maybe sometime in your past or in a dream or in
a vision or something, somebody told you about the
Okies. Maybe one of your editors or producers had a
whiff of the story."

"They had no whiffs. They let me run with it because they trust me. I just told them it was so and that
was it. That's how it works. It's how it works. Those
people don't have whiffs. All they have is ears to hear
my voice and mouths to say it's too high for an anchorman's so that means, sorry, Arch, you stay where
you are forever."

He turned around to me like he was going to cry.
"I have to figure this thing out. I have to figure out
what to do. Please leave me alone now."

"Certainly. Everything I have said here tonight is
on the record, by the way, except about the wiretap.
You can't use that."

"Just go, please."

I let myself out of his room, rode the elevator down
to the lobby, went to my car and drove to the rendez-
vous spot.

I was almost feeling a tiny bit sorry for Archibald
Tyler, CBS News, Oklahoma City. Almost. Brother
Walt had been right. As usual. It had nothing to do

with money. It had to do with a voice that squeaked like a closing screen door.

C. was there in the parking lot just beyond the Santa Fe train station on Sheridan. He was there with Brother Walt and an Oklahoma Blue Arrow Motorcoaches GMC. The bus was like the one Tyler and I sat in at the Ardmore bus station. I had no idea how C. had managed to commandeer such a thing on such short notice in the middle of the night. And I hadn't asked.

Brother Walt was not pleased about his plane ride.

"I have got a lot of arrangements to cancel now," I said to him. "We were going to bring the Oklahoma City Symphony and maybe Billy Graham and my old friends Roy Rogers and Dale Evans for the funeral. Now we won't need them. You are alive. Too bad. It would have been some show."

"It's still a lunatic way to move from place to place, Mack. No way God meant people to get in that big a hurry. There is always time to drive or ride a train or bus."

"Quick. Give me the scripture where God says it's okay to ride trains and buses but no planes. Quick, now. Is it in Ecclesiastes? . . ."

C., still new to the relationship between Brother Walt and me, stepped between us.

"Sorry to interrupt talk about God, gents, but there's a psycho reporter to take care of over at the Park Plaza. Shouldn't we review what's supposed to happen?"

We reviewed what was supposed to happen, and at 11:24 climbed aboard the bus. The driver was OBI agent Smitty, dressed in the two-tone gray uniform of an Oklahoma Blue Arrow Motorcoaches driver. He looked like the real thing, except for not having a ticket punch in a holder on his hip. He apparently felt he would have no need for a ticket punch tonight.

"Did you steal this bus?" I asked C.

"No. I prayed for it and God delivered," he said.

"Jokes about God are my territory, Mr. Director," said Brother Walt sternly. "They are off limits to everybody but preachers."

It was clear C. didn't know if Brother Walt was kidding or not. Neither did I. The man would always be a puzzle to me. A lovely, loving, brilliant puzzle.

Brother Walt had dressed the way we agreed. He had on a white dress shirt open at the collar with a dark blue suit coat and a pair of gray slacks. On his head was a broad-brimmed western hat made out of tan felt. On his feet were western boots. On his eyes was a pair of heavy-rimmed light-lens sunglasses.

He took a seat two-thirds of the way back in the bus. C. and I, also wearing sunglasses, went all the way to the back.

Smitty put the GMC—bus people call them Jimmys—in gear and eased it away from the curb for the five-block trip to the Park Plaza.

"Is he going to be there?" C. asked as we sat down.

"Yes, sir," I replied. "I'd bet the store on it."

"I think you already have," Brother Walt boomed back at us. "But you can relax, Mack. I'm sure Jackie'll give you a job running one of her stores if this blows up in your face."

"What about you, Reverend?" I asked.

"I work for God and this is God's work I am doing here on this bus tonight."

"Wish I worked for a boss like that," C. said.

"Come see me in Adabel when this is over and I'll get you ordained."

"Pass."

I heard the lovely swishing sound of the Jimmy's air brakes. Smitty turned the corner and eased the bus

up into the circle driveway in front of the Park Plaza
Hotel.

Okay, Tyler. Where are you?

There he was. Standing just inside the revolving
door.

"He's coming," I said quietly to my colleagues on
the bus.

Smitty opened the bus door. Tyler walked outside
and climbed up into the entry stairwell.

Brother Walt boomed out: "Walk toward the rear of
the bus, Mr. Tyler. Count four rows on the left-hand
side and sit down in the aisle seat."

Tyler tried to see who was talking. The bus was
dark. He might have been able to see a rough outline
of Brother Walt, alias Boomer. C. and I were lying
down on our seats, just to make sure he never saw us.
A glimpse of Brother Walt/Boomer was all we wanted
him to see.

"Do as I say, Mr. Tyler. Do it or I'll have the driver
remove you from this bus and this whole thing is
over," Brother Walt said. His voice and manner were
perfect. He was definitely Boomer, head of the criminal gang called the Okies. Definitely.

"I want to see who I'm talking to," Tyler said.

"Then get yourself off this bus!" Brother Walt's
voice was so loud I swear I heard windows rattle in
the bus. He overdid it just a bit.

"All right, all right," said Tyler. And he went to
the fourth aisle seat and sat down with his back to
Brother Walt and the rear of the bus.

"Now, listen up, Mr. Tyler. Listen up to what I am
now going to tell you. I plan to tell it only once and
only to you. There will be no more interviews, no
more statements. Got it?"

There was silence from Tyler.

"All right then," Brother Walt continued. "I am

Boomer. I am the founder and leader of the Okies. How you found out about me and us, I do not know. You will now tell me, Mr. Tyler.''

"Forget it, Mr. Whoeveryouare," Tyler said in a voice that was wavering. Could be from more drink. Could be from severe nervousness. "You people don't exist and you know it. I don't know what's going on. . . ."

"Who's our rat?" Brother Walt yelled. "I want the name of the Okie fink who squealed to you! I want it now!"

"This is nuts. Nobody told me anything. I made it up."

"You didn't make me up. You didn't make up me and my boys. You think I'm stupid enough to fall for that? I want the name of your source."

"For Chrissake, listen to me! There is no source!"

"No need to profane the name of Our Lord and Savior."

My throat and my brain tightened. You blew it, Brother Walt! You just blew the whole thing!

"Don't tell me you are a preacher in addition to being a notorious crime boss," said Tyler.

"God works in mysterious ways," said Brother Walt. I could feel him ducking and weaving. He knew he was in trouble.

"You're telling me God told you to go out and steal from people?"

"God does not speak directly to the likes of me," said Brother Walt. "I am a sinner now, but I have not always been a sinner. I grew up in the home of a preacher. He was a man of God, but it didn't take. But I do remember some of the lingo. That's all."

Not bad, Brother Walt.

"The worst kid in my high school was a Methodist preacher's son," Tyler said. "He used to drive over to Joplin, Missouri, all the time and buy whiskey. I know the type. There's a bad preacher's kid in every school. At least one.''

Made it.

Tyler coughed. He had been smoking since he sat down. I could smell the smoke. I had never noticed him smoking before. The pressure was taking.

"Cigarettes will kill you," Brother Walt said. "You want something cold to drink?"

"Sure. You got something back there?" Tyler coughed again. And again.

"Driver, stop at the first place you see where we can get this poor dying man a Dr Pepper," Brother Walt yelled up to Smitty.

I felt the bus slowing down.

"I hate Dr Pepper," Tyler said.

"Well, then what pleases you?"

"Grapette."

Grapette! It must be the Kansas background. Good for you, Archibald Tyler, CBS News, Oklahoma City. Anybody who likes Grapette can't be all bad. Rah, rah, Jayhawk!

I heard the sound of the Jimmy's air brakes. We were coming to a stop.

"Yes, sir, right here is fine," Brother Walt said. "I hear these JackieMarts are wonderful places. You just drive up and get what you want without having to get out of the car."

How about that? Smitty figured to keep it all in the family. It had to be JackieMart–South Western. I knew the route Smitty was supposed to be driving.

I heard him say into the order box: "One Grapette, please." Then came the voice of one of Jackie's employees: "Thank you. Drive to pick-up window two. Your order will be ready. It'll be forty-eight cents. Thank you."

It was Tommy Walt's voice! What was he doing taking orders here now? What's going on?

The bus moved again. I remembered the discussion Jackie had with the carpenters who did the building. She wanted the drive-up canopies to be tall enough and wide enough to accommodate trucks and buses as well as cars. That was one smart woman I was married to.

I heard an exchange of thank yous between Smitty and a young man I was now certain had to be Tommy Walt. I was sure Smitty got a receipt for the forty-eight cents. Somehow the Grapette got to Tyler. I couldn't see if Smitty took it back to him or what. The whole thing made me thirsty for one myself.

The bus moved again.

"You feeling better now, Mr. Tyler?" Brother Walt asked.

"Sure. Fine. Thanks."

"Now let me give you your story. You listening?"

Tyler did not reply. Brother Walt went on. Maybe Tyler held up his hand or the Grapette.

"The story is this. We're through. Your fink and your stories and all that has flowed from that has sent my people running for cover. Some are singing to the state cops. Most ran off to Texas. Others are in New Mexico. One even went to Arkansas, that's how bad it is. It's done. We're through. And I don't want any more stories about us. You hear me? You hear me loud and well and clear?"

There was no answer.

"You caught us. How you caught us, I don't know, but you caught us. My people were a lot more chicken than I thought. Oklahoma is too small to get really lost in. We're through. Thanks to you, we're through. Congratulations."

Brother Walt let it sit for a while. We rode in silence

for what seemed like several minutes but was probably only a minute or two.

"I'm taking you back to the hotel, Mr. Tyler. I'm tired of talking to you. You are obviously a man who does not know what's right or what's smart for himself."

"Will you let me interview you on film?"

Bull's-eye!

"No way. No way at all. You're getting off this bus and I'm disappearing forever."

"What if we kept the lights off and people couldn't see your face?"

"Forget it. You heard what I said here. Just quote that."

"I'm in the television business. I need pictures."

"Make them up."

Tyler laughed. He coughed. And laughed and laughed. And coughed.

Then the bus stopped.

"Out!" yelled Brother Walt.

I heard the sounds of Tyler walking down the aisle of the bus and down the steps and out.

Smitty closed the door, gunned the motor and drove off.

"God is Great!" Brother Walt yelled.

In a few more seconds, after the bus turned a corner, Smitty yelled, "Clear!"

I sat up. So did C. Brother Walt was standing over us in the middle of the aisle.

"Did it work? The answer is yes," said Brother Walt.

"Couldn't help being a preacher, could you?" I said.

"It's automatic after all these years. Somebody uses the name in vain and I react. Sorry."

"I think you pulled it out. We'll see pretty soon if it all really worked."

We made arrangements for early morning and said our good-byes back at the train station where our cars were parked.

It was 12:15—fifteen minutes after midnight.

C. went off in his Lincoln. Brother Walt got in the Buick with me. He was going to spend the night with us.

Jackie was at the front door waiting for us. She gave Brother Walt a huge hug and me a kiss and then said, "Well?" She was fully dressed and her eyes were aglow. It was clear something else was up that didn't have a thing to do with the Okies.

"Well, we'll know in the morning," I said. "Brother Walt was a dynamite Boomer. Great acting job."

"God is Great," he said. "Now I must go up to bed. I assume I am in the back guest room."

"You assume correctly," Jackie said.

He left and I looked at Jackie as if we should follow. I had agreed to be at C.'s OBI office at 6:30. She grabbed my arm and whispered, "Tommy Walt needs to talk to you. He's in the kitchen."

"Jackie, please. I know he was at the South Western store tonight. I'd love to know why, but I have had an incredible day and night. I've got to be up at six. . . ."

"He's had an incredible night, too. He must talk to you. He has an announcement."

"What kind of announcement?"

She shrugged, I shrugged, and we went into the kitchen.

Tommy Walt was still in his blue and white Buses uniform. He jumped to his feet.

"Did Mom tell you?" he said.

"No, she didn't." I sat down across the table from him. Jackie went over to the sink to stand and watch.

His hands were shaking. Here was my son and he was afraid to tell me what he was about to tell me. What in the world had he done? Held up a gas station? Bombed the bus station? Is there a girl pregnant? Is he joining the Marines?

"I'm giving up baseball, Dad." There were tears in his eyes. And suddenly there were some in mine too. I glanced over at Jackie. Her eyes were as dry as the panhandle.

"It is not my game," Tommy Walt said. "I couldn't make it at second base, I couldn't make it at the plate, and I can't make it on the mound. I can't stand being called Trash. I am not trash. I love watching and following the game, but I can't play it anymore. I just can't. Please try to understand."

The boy was in pain. Serious pain. I wanted to touch him. It had been a while since I had done that. Fathers just don't reach over and touch sons after they get to be fifteen years old, the way they ought to. I'll never forget that my own dad, bless his heart, never did that when I lost my eye. There I was, losing my dream of being a Kansas highway patrolman like him, and he did not hug me or touch me in any way. Now here I was, not doing the same thing to my own son. He hadn't lost an eye, but he was hurting almost as badly as if he had.

"Son, it does not matter," I said. And I meant it. I really did. "I am proud of you the way you have hung in there all these years. I am truly proud. Where is it written down that every young man in Oklahoma and America has to play baseball all his life?"

I reached over and touched his hand. He grabbed it like he was about to go underwater for the third and last time. "Thanks, Dad. I know you have been disappointed. I know you wanted me to be Stan Musial, Car Two. . . ."

"There's only one Stan the Man and there's only one you. I like Tommy Walt, Car One, just the way you are."

"Thanks, Dad."

I looked up at the clock right above Jackie's head and the kitchen sink. It was almost one o'clock. "Well, I've got to be up again in five hours. . . ."

"There's one more thing, Dad," he said. "I've quit the bus business too. I just hate it at the bus station. I know you love bus stations, but I don't. Everybody calls me Trash. I'm sorry, but I just couldn't bear to work there with all the guys after I quit the team anyhow. Especially Glisan."

"He's going to miss you."

"No, he isn't. I called him after the game tonight and told him I was through. All he said, was, 'Have a good bat at life wherever you go, Trash. Does your father know?' "

"Who won tonight?"

"They did, of course. The final score was eight to zip. We never scored a run. I was the official losing pitcher, of course. It was the worst night ever, Dad. You were there. You and Mom saw it."

"Forget all of that, son. We'll talk tomorrow about where we might be able to find you another job."

"That's already been taken care of, Dad. It's the other part of the announcement. I'm going into the business with Mom. I'm going to manage JackieMart–South Western."

I turned around to Jackie. She was smiling and nodding. "I finally took your advice, Mack. I fired T. Ray Powell tonight. He wasn't cut out for drive-thru grocery work. Wrong kind of nerves."

"But I am cut out for it, Dad," Tommy Walt said. "I filled in there this evening and I loved it. The chal-

lenge is to see how fast you can get those orders together. There are only a few seconds between the time
the order is given and the time the customer arrives at
the pick-up window. Tonight we filled a sixteen-item
order in less than thirty seconds. I think I can get that
down to twenty-five or even twenty. Some of the items
need to be organized a little differently, is all."

"Maybe after a little training, he can open up number
four completely on his own on the northwest side,"
said Jackie with pride and enthusiasm. "There's a spot
on Northwest Highway I'm looking at that might be
perfect. He could be my first franchisee. Good way to
test the idea. Then we can move on to Lawton and
Atoka and all the other places in Oklahoma and the
world that want JackieMarts."

She abruptly stopped talking. She and Tommy Walt
were both staring at me. Is he going to explode like a
volcano? Is he going to weep? Scream? Curse? Is he
going to turn over the table? Throw something?

"Well, congratulations all around," I said.

I stood up and Tommy Walt stood up. I hugged him
just like he was ten instead of twenty-one. Then I went
over and grabbed Jackie. She was crying now.

"I thought you'd be upset," she said. "I thought
you'd think it was embarrassing or something that a son
goes into business with his mother."

"Jackie and Son Mart has a nice ring to it," I said.
"Hard to bring a son into the lieutenant governor's
business anyhow, you know."

"You're a wonderful man, Mack," she said.

"I'm happy for both of you. I am really happy," I said.

And it was true.

Almost.

13

Crown Oklahoma, Mack

I had never before set foot in the offices of the Oklahoma Bureau of Investigation. They were in a one-story building up at 36th Street and Eastern next to the headquarters of the state highway patrol. I had somehow expected C. to have a huge office with framed pictures of J. Edgar Hoover, Eliot Ness and other lawman notables on the walls. Instead he worked out of space that wasn't much bigger than the one I had as lieutenant governor. The only picture on the wall was a map of the Oklahoma Territory as drawn by some U.S. Government surveyor in 1842 before the land rush. That's when the Oklahoma Indian Territory was opened on a first-come basis for land claims and settlement. The Sooners were the guys who cheated and snuck over the night before.

C. was bright-eyed, all in his starch and gray just like he had had ten hours of sleep instead of five. He took me into a room behind an unmarked gray door.

"Nobody, but nobody, knows about this," he said

again and again. "It is our secret. It must remain a secret, Mack. Always."

I repeated what I had told him eight or nine times already. My lips were sealed. Politicians could threaten me, crooks could torture me, reporters could bribe me, and I would never, ever squeal on his telephone-tapping setup. I also recalled what Dad said about secrets. But I did the recalling only to myself.

Smitty and one other man were manning the machines when we walked into the room. It was a simple operation. There were a couple of sophisticated-looking tape recorders and five or six telephones and stacks of used and unused tapes.

"Nothing yet," Smitty said.

C. and I took seats in two wooden chairs in the back of the small room.

"Bad sign, Mack," C. said. "I figure he should have been on the phone already."

"He was up late last night too, remember. Maybe he's a late sleeper. . . ."

Then it began to happen. Smitty raised his right hand. He pointed to a loudspeaker up to his right over the bank of telephones. Through it came the voice of a woman.

"Good morning, Braniff International," she said. "May I help you?"

A high-pitched male voice responded: "Yes. I need to cancel on your seven thirty-five flight this morning to Washington-Dulles. The name's Tyler. A. Tyler."

There was a two-beat pause. "Thank you, Mr. Tyler, for calling. It is too bad more people aren't as thoughtful as you and don't cancel. It would certainly help us help others get seats on our flights. Failure to cancel leads to overbooking and to underbooking and the end result . . ."

"Glad I could make your day so early." He hung up.

C. gave me a thumbs-up and a grin. Which I returned.

Nothing happened for five minutes. Or ten minutes. Or fifteen minutes.

Then Smitty took a call on a dark blue phone. He listened and took some notes.

He turned around to C. and me.

"The person in question ordered a room service breakfast of orange juice, coffee and two Danish rolls. The room service waiter who delivered them said the person in question was fully dressed except for a suit coat and tie and was typing on a typewriter set upon a table. He said the room was full of cigarette smoke and the ashtrays were full of cigarette butts. That's it."

"Good news," I said to C.

"Precisely. Also, maybe he'll smoke himself to death and we'll be through with him that way," C. said.

We were served our own breakfast of coffee and chocolate-covered cake doughnuts.

A good twenty minutes went by. It was now almost eight o'clock. Nine o'clock on the East Coast, C. reminded me.

Smitty raised his right hand and pointed again to the speaker.

"CBS News," said a young man's voice.

Tyler identified himself and asked for Greg Upshaw. In a second to two Greg Upshaw, whom we knew to be the CBS Washington bureau chief, was on the line. I was barely breathing. This was it. Up or down, win or lose. We found out right now.

"Bulletin, Greg," Tyler said. "I got an exclusive with the real Boomer last night."

"Jesus Murphy! On film?"

"No. He wouldn't do that. But I talked to him. He hasn't talked to anybody else. And he won't talk to anybody else. He's ours. Forever."

"Fab-u-lous. What's he say?"

"He says it's all over. We blew it up and away. I've got it confirmed by the lieutenant governor too. He's the clown in charge of the investigation for the State of Oklahoma. I'm sure he will sit down for some sound. Only has one eye. Wears a patch. Right out of a shirt commercial. A bit on the weird side, but smart. Originally from Kansas."

"Fab-u-lous."

"I'll do a stand-upper from in front of the capitol again. We'll have it to you for tonight."

"Fab-u-lous. I can hardly wait to tell Roger. There's nothing else in sight right now. Probably lead the broadcast. Good work, Arch. Damned fine work."

"Thank you, sir. Thank you very much."

"What about that big deal you wanted to see me about this morning?"

"It passed. It was nothing."

C. gave me thumbs up. I held up the middle finger on my right hand to the loudspeaker in order to send a silent message to Archibald Tyler, CBS News, Oklahoma City.

"Did you notice the guy didn't ask one question to test to see if Tyler really talked to a Boomer?" C. said. "He just took his word for it. What a crazy way to do business."

"Precisely."

I took Brother Walt to the bus depot so he could catch the 1:15 Continental Trailways back to Adabel. He wasn't about to fly back on C.'s Cessna 207 Skywagon.

"A man is a fool who does what he knows is wrong a second time after escaping with body and soul the first time," he said.

I told him that sounded more like what Confucius would say than Jesus Christ, Our Lord and Savior. He said it was in the Book of John and I could look it up if I did not believe him. I did not believe him, but I did not look it up.

"I would hate to think what my life would be like without you," I told him on the loading dock. They had already given his bus a first call. "I seem to be always saying thank you to you."

"You are really thanking God," he said. "We are all here to do God's work. Turning you a hand now and then is God's work."

"God is Great," I replied.

Hugh B. Glisan would not let me leave the depot without a few words. A few lousy words. Trash was a good boy, he said. He would miss him, even if he did go berserk a time or two.

"The bus business is a peculiar business," he said. "Not everybody is cut out for it. It takes a particular kind of person. It's just like with you, I guess. Not everybody is cut out to be lieutenant governor of Oklahoma the way you are, sir. The important thing is for Trash not to think of himself as a failure because he couldn't cut it in the bus business and had to go to work for his mother at a drive-in grocery store."

"I'll be sure and tell him that," I said. "Thank you, Glisan."

Dad went back to Kansas on what used to be the Santa Fe's Texas Chief. Now run by something called Amtrak, trains were a long way from being what they used to be, but they were still his favorite way to travel. The Texas Chief in particular had a special place for me, because it was on that train that I met Pepper after I ran off from Kansas to Texas. We rode it together to Galveston and became best friends.

Dad had spent two days holed up alone in the Holiday Inn after he did his NBC interview. He was to await further instructions from us, which never came because there was no need to do anything else.

"This sure beats chasing speeders and bootleggers through Kansas," he said at the train station. "Call me anytime. That's what dads of lieutenant governor sons are for."

I thought for a second he might reach over and embrace me. Nope. Never had, never would.

I decided right then that I would go home that night and hug Tommy Walt again. And I did. Much to his surprise and embarrassment. He had had a great first day as manager of JackieMart–South Western, having quickly reduced order-filling time by putting the bread right next to the milk refrigerator rather than with the rest of the baked goods. So many people wanted those together and now it was possible for an employee to grab both at the same time.

I thought it would be proper and smart for C. and me to go in and brief the governor on what was going on. It took me a while to convince Buffalo Joe's secretary we were there to deliver good news. He was on his way to make a speech in Tonkawa and was not in the mood for anything sour today, she said. Today or any other day, I did not say.

"Just got three minutes, three minutes before I'm due to hotfoot it out of here," he said, shaking our hands and patting our backs like he was supposed to do. "Sylvia said you have some good news?"

"The best," I said. "The Okies story ends tonight. They've come and gone. CBS will report their departure tonight. Quoting Boomer and me."

"You? You?"

"Yes, sir."

"Normally, major good news like this should come from this office, don't you think, Mack? What about that, Mack? Doesn't good news normally get announced by this office?"

"Normally, yes, Joe. But this is not normally. C. and I had a little plan going and it meant that I had to say some very specific things. . . ."

Buffalo Joe held up a hand. Silence. "Forget it. Forget it. You may be the governor of this state in two weeks anyhow, Mack." He gave me a wink. Then he remembered C. was standing there with me. "You keep a secret, C.?"

"Secrets are my business," C. said. "Secrets are my business."

"Gentlemen," said Buffalo Joe, "they're thinking about, they're thinking about me—us—for the Cabinet. For the Cabinet. Secretary of agriculture. They're looking for a Democrat. There are eighteen on the list. Eighteen on the list. Under your hat now. Way, way under your hat. Getting rid of the Okies could help matters. Yes, indeed. If we got to the Cabinet, where does that mean we go next? Check me for the tan, Mack. Check me for the tan. And where would you go if we go, Mack? Right into this office as First Man of Oklahoma, that is where. From Second Man to First Man, Mack, right into this office. But you must promise me one thing, Mack. You must build the dome. You must. The people of this state want it, the people of this state deserve it. You must Crown Oklahoma, Mack. Crown it with a revolving restaurant if you can. If you can. That is my preference. I haven't said it until now, but that is my preference. A revolving restaurant."

"I'll do my best, Joe," I said.

"Got to run for a plane. We hope to Texas hell you never see anything like this Okies business on TV again," Joe said as he moved toward the door. There was a touch of rebuke for me in his voice.

"I hope so too, Joe."

"Come to think of it, why don't you take a break from watching TV till this Cabinet thing is worked out. No point in taking any risks. No point at all."

"Will do, Joe."

"Crown Oklahoma, Mack." And he was gone from his own office.

"How about making that revolving restaurant a Burger King?" C. said. "Crown Oklahoma with a Burger King, Mack."

Two weeks later, the president of the United States chose another of the eighteen to be secretary of agriculture. A Republican congressman from Minnesota. So Buffalo Joe Hayman remained a Democrat and governor, and I remained lieutenant governor.

The hour I spent with Archibald Tyler that final morning was both the most delicious and the most disgusting I have ever spent with another human being. We heard his call for an appointment on Smitty's speaker. Janice Alice said she would get back to him as soon as she could. He said he wanted to come at 10:30. I waited a few minutes and called her to see if there were any messages. She told me of Tyler's request and I said fine.

I recognized the film crew as the same one that was with him in Ardmore the day Boomer Webster was blown to bits. They set up their camera in my office. I told Tyler on camera the same things I had told him the night before in his hotel room. We had the Okies under control. Several were in custody. Others had fled the state. We believed their illegal activities were halted in our state—if not elsewhere as well. "They apparently couldn't stand the heat from the light," I said. A good line.

As the camera crew got their equipment together afterward, I walked casually to the front door of my office with Tyler. I wanted to say: Clown? You think I'm a clown, do you? Well, let me tell you something. You have just been had, Mr. Archibald Tyler. You have been faked clean out of your socks, Mr. Archibald Tyler. And guess who did it to you, Mr. Tyler? That weird one-eyed lieutenant governor you think is a clown. If he's a clown, Mr. Tyler, what does that make you?

All I said was: "Hope you return to our state on a more pleasant assignment in the future."

"Sure," was all he said, his voice as high as ever, his future in television news as cramped as ever because of it.

He had that look on his face. That look people get sometimes when they wonder if what they saw was real. When they're trying to figure out what really did happen. When they're having big, big second thoughts about something. It usually happens right after they wrote a check for closing costs on a house. Or signed the papers to buy a new Chrysler Imperial. Or walked away from an altar married to a girl who makes her own clothes.

"I meant that about sending some money to the Boomer Webster fund," he said. "Due to the new circumstances, I will not be able to send as much as I might have otherwise, but a check will be sent. I promise. Maybe I can get CBS to throw in a few bucks too."

I smiled and said that would be just grand.

C. had been waiting in an adjoining office. We watched Tyler and his crew disappear down the hallway toward the grand staircase that would take them out of the domeless state capitol building of our Sooner State of Oklahoma.

"Will he try it again on another story sometime, Mack?" C. asked.

"Probably," I said. "If he doesn't, another one will. It's too easy."

C. said, "Thank God you were here to stop it this time, Mr. One-Eyed Mack."

"Thank God *you* were, Mr. One-Eared C."

"How did you lose that eye?" he said.

"It happened when I was sixteen and a half. I was outside watching some little kids play kick-the-can. One of them kicked the can up in my face and the ragged lid caught my left eye and tore it out."

"Then that baseball story going around is a crock?"

"Yes, sir. How about your ear?"

"I was on a police pistol range down in Durant when I was a rookie cop, and some idiot next to me got too close with a forty-five and shot my ear off."

"So the Nazi prison story going around is a crock?"

"Precisely. Why don't you wear a glass eye?"

"Why don't you wear a glass ear?"

We both laughed. We shook hands.

"I hope I never have to investigate you, Mack," he said. "I hope I never have to investigate you, Mack."

"Me too," I said. "Me too."

About the Author

Jim Lehrer, associate editor of *The MacNeil/Lehrer NewsHour* on PBS, was born in Kansas and grew up there and in Texas. He was a Trailways ticket agent, a Marine, and a newspaperman before joining public television. Of Lehrer's five novels, CROWN OKLAHOMA is the second concerning The One-Eyed Mack. Lehrer also writes plays. He is married to the novelist Kate Lehrer; they have three daughters and live in Washington, DC.